Mail Order Midnight

A Brides of Beckham Story

Kirsten Osbourne

Chapter One

Constance groaned as she heard the pounding on her door. She must have missed the rooster's crow again. She hated mornings with a passion, but her mother insisted she be up as soon at dawn so she could have breakfast and do her chores.

The door opened. "Constance Jane Dailey! You've overslept again. Why are you so lazy?"

Constance didn't argue with her mother because she knew it would be futile. She did tell herself she wasn't lazy though. Sleeping later than most didn't make you lazy. No, it was sitting around doing nothing that made you lazy. And Constance was always doing something to contribute. She just wished her day could start a little later. She didn't see the crime!

"I'm getting up," Constance said, swinging her feet to the floor. "I'll be out in a minute." She thought for the millionth time that she needed to marry, but she needed to marry a man who thought days should begin later than sunup. Not that she'd ever met that sort of man or even believed he existed.

Her mother shut the door, and Constance yawned. She put on her everyday dress and headed outside to the outhouse.

When she was back inside, she sat down to breakfast. Her two younger siblings were already there, most of their meal gone. "This looks delicious. Thanks, Ma."

"How late were you up last night?" her pa asked, frowning at her.

"I went for a walk late. Probably shortly after midnight."

He shook his head. "Why would you stay up so late, knowing you were needed up at dawn to help around the farm?"

Constance looked down at her food, shrugging. "I just feel like I'm on a time clock different than everyone else's. You all look so happy in the mornings, and I want to throw rotten eggs at anyone who speaks to me. Late at night is glorious. The world feels so pure, as if there are no people around to mess it up. You know?"

Her ma took her spot at the table. "You need coffee."

"I don't *like* coffee," Constance told her mother for the millionth time. "I do as much work as everyone else. I just start a little later and work a little harder."

"Not under my roof you don't." Pa glared at her.

"Yes, sir," Constance replied, knowing full well they'd be having the same conversation again. Soon. She wished there was someone who understood her need to stay up late and sleep later in the day.

As soon as breakfast was over and Johnny and Mary were off to school, Ma handed Constance a basket and a list. "Walk into town, buy everything on the list, and check at the post office for our mail."

Constance nodded. "Yes, Ma." She really did like shopping days because she could wander along the road, thinking about things as she moved. She loved walks in the same way she loved staying up all night.

The walk that morning was heavenly. It was spring, and the flowers were blooming all around her. Summer was coming, and though Constance didn't hate winter the way some did, she was happy it was spring. It meant the whole world was renewed and there would be baby animals.

Once she reached town, she went straight to the general store, getting everything on her ma's list. Ma was always very meticulous as she explained exactly what she wanted on her lists. It amused Constance to find the things her mother wanted.

After putting the supplies on her father's account, she walked to the post office. A woman she had heard many things about stood in line ahead of her. "Are you still sending mail order brides out west?" Constance asked without forethought. She hadn't planned to ask, but now that she had, she realized it may be her way out. She could go west, marry a stranger, and perhaps she could even find one who didn't mind sleeping late.

The woman—Elizabeth Tandy—nodded. "I am. Are you looking for a husband?"

"Not hard enough, according to my mother." Constance grinned. "Any chance there's a man who works at night and wouldn't mind if his wife slept in til eight?"

Elizabeth smiled. "I just got a letter from a man yesterday who drives a freight wagon in his local area. He's in South Dakota, and he works odd hours. He said he needed a wife who didn't feel the need to adhere to a rigid schedule."

"That would be me. Tell him that's me, would you?"

"You should tell him yourself. Do you have time to stop by on your way home?" Elizabeth asked.

Constance shook her head. "No, my mother thinks all work for the day should be completed by noon. Can I come by after lunch?"

"Of course. Any time you can find to come by within the next few days would be great."

"Thank you so much!"

Elizabeth took her turn receiving mail and then Constance was requesting her family's. "Anything for Dailey?" she asked.

The postmistress handed Constance two letters. "Thank you."

Constance hurried home, practically running, so she could finish her chores on time. On her mother's time of course, and then she could visit Elizabeth that afternoon. She'd need to sweep, dust, and help with the noon meal if her mother asked. Other than that, she was finished with her chores for the day.

She put the supplies onto the worktable, and her mother looked through them quickly. "You got everything just right."

Constance smiled. With the way her mother's lists were, it was impossible to get the wrong thing.

Constance quickly did her chores and had them finished well before her mother asked for help with the meal. It was only Constance,

Ma, and Pa who ate the noon meal together during the week. Johnny and Mary would stay at school and eat the lunches they'd taken.

As soon as the meal was over, Constance sprang to her feet to wash the dishes before her mother even had a chance to ask. When they were wiped and put away, Constance removed her apron. "Is it all right if I visit a friend this afternoon?" Constance hated feeling as if she had to ask. She was nineteen years old! Most of her friends were already married.

"Yes, that's fine."

Constance kissed her mother's cheek before turning to run off. "Thanks, Ma!" she called over her shoulder.

As she hurried, she thought about actually stepping inside the house where Elizabeth lived with her husband. Her home was huge, one of the largest in town, and it was fancy. She was excited to see inside it, but she was even more excited at the idea of marrying a man who didn't like rigid schedules. Oh, she couldn't wait.

Once she got to Rock Creek Road, she knocked loudly. She was invited to be there, and she was proud of that fact.

The door was opened by the man she recognized as Elizabeth's husband. "I have an appointment with Mrs. Tandy," she said.

"Yes, of course." He led her through the house to a room where Elizabeth sat at a desk. "You have a visitor."

Elizabeth looked up and nodded, smiling at her husband. "Thank you."

"I'll check on the children. Take your time," Mr. Tandy shut the door as he left the room.

"Let me find the letter I told you about. You can read it and respond if you are interested in marrying the man."

Constance took the letter offered to her. "It seems odd to just read a letter to decide if a man is right for me."

"I'm sure it does." Elizabeth smiled. "But I do this all the time, and I've never sent a woman who was unhappy with her marriage."

Unfolding the letter, Constance started to read.

Dear Matchmaker,

I am a thirty-year-old man who lives just outside Sioux Falls, South Dakota. I drive freight for a living, and I tend to be gone most evenings. I would like a bride who would not be bothered by the hours I keep, and who would be flexible enough to not adhere to a rigid schedule.

If you could find a woman like that for me, I would be the happiest man alive. I make a good living for myself, and I'm ready to start a family. Please find someone who has these traits.

Looks don't matter to me, but I would be especially happy if she had long brown hair.

I'm enclosing money for your fee and a train ticket into Sioux Falls. Thank you for your assistance.

Leonard Berry

Constance read through the letter again. "He's perfect. I'll take him." She even had long brown hair like he'd requested. They were a match made in heaven. She hoped.

Elizabeth laughed. "I'll send him a telegram with the day and time of your arrival. When do you want to leave?"

Constance pursed her lips, thinking about how hard it would be to tell her family what she'd decided to do. "Monday," she said. That would give her five days to explain and pack all her belongings.

"All right. I'll see about getting your ticket and let Mr. Berry know when you'll arrive." Elizabeth grinned. "I'm glad you decided to go to him. I think you both need a match who can live alternate hours."

"Alternate hours. I like that!" Constance got to her feet. "I'll go home and explain now. That's going to be the hard part."

"It always is," Elizabeth said with a smile. "Many of my siblings have gone to be brides—or grooms. It'll work out. I promise."

On her way home, Constance went over and over in her mind what she should say to her mother. She knew Ma would be disappointed in her decision. She could just feel it in her bones. Hopefully, through her disappointment, her mother would understand why she needed to do this. She wouldn't dare mention the alternate hours thing, though. Her mother would never be able to understand why Constance wasn't fond of mornings.

When Constance walked onto the farm a short while later, her mother was hanging clothes. It was a task they usually did together, so Constance joined her to help. "I didn't know you were planning to do wash this afternoon."

"I wasn't. Farmer's almanac says rain tomorrow, so your pa asked me to do it a day early."

Constance looked off into the distance. It didn't look like rain was coming, and the Farmer's Almanac was wrong as often as it was right. "I see," Constance said, though she didn't. The way her parents did things confused her at times. "I went to see Elizabeth Tandy today."

Ma nodded. "Isn't she the one who sends women out west to marry strangers?"

"She is. And I've agreed to be one of those women."

Ma stopped what she was doing, one hand raised in the air, a clothespin clutched in that hand. "What made you decide to do that?"

Constance shrugged. "I don't exactly have any suitors right now, and I thought it was time I married and raised a family."

"You're a pretty girl. We could find you someone."

"No need. I'm going to South Dakota. Doesn't that sound exciting?"

Ma shrugged. "I guess when you're young and longing for adventure any place can seem exciting. When do you leave?"

Surprised at how well her mother was taking the news, Constance said, "Monday."

"You never have been one to let moss grow, have you?" Ma sighed. "Let me tell your father. He'll take it better from me."

"So...you don't have a problem with me doing this?"

Ma shook her head. "No, I don't. I think it's time you chose your own path in life."

Constance dropped the dress she was holding into the laundry basket between them and threw her arms around her mother. "Thank you, Ma!"

Ma patted her awkwardly. "Just be happy, Constance."

"I will do my best!"

As soon as laundry was finished, she and ma went through her clothes. "I do wish you'd given us an extra week to make you a dress to be married in."

"I think with that sewing machine of yours, we could have it done before Monday with no problem. Mary can do the cooking for a few days."

Ma looked at her for a moment before nodding. "She really can. We've taught her well. That means another trip into town for you in the morning. You'll need to buy some fabric, and we'll make that dress. It won't be easy, but I don't need easy."

Constance smiled. "I don't either."

And just like that, her mother was helping her get ready for a marriage that would take her far away.

They continued to go through her clothes, putting stuff in piles. "We should have done this a long time ago," Constance said. "I think these two dresses would fit Mary."

Soon all her clothes were sorted by those she should take, those she should pass on to her sister, and those that should be discarded for rags.

After supper, Constance went for a walk, looking at the stars. It was her favorite thing to do at night, but this time she had an ulterior motive. It would give her parents time to talk so her father could learn of the wedding in the best way possible.

Mary joined Constance, something she did on rare occasions. "Thank you for the dresses," she said. "I've been wondering how much longer the ones I have would fit over my bosoms."

Constance smiled. "I'm happy to give them to you. Ma and I are making me a new dress this weekend, so you'll have to take care of cooking."

Mary shrugged. "It's good practice for me. At least that's what Ma would say."

"You're a good cook. You just have to remember that and not second-guess yourself."

"That's much harder in practice," Mary said, sighing. "I always think I've messed something up, and I try to fix it, and I ruin it by trying to fix it. It's silly of me, but I do it every time."

"This time, you shouldn't," Constance said.

"What's going on, Connie?" Mary asked. "What are Ma and Pa whispering about?"

"I've decided to go west as a mail-order bride."

"You're marrying a stranger?" Mary sounded shocked.

"I am. I have no marriage prospects here. It's time I married and started a family of my own. This just feels right. Ma is telling Pa for me."

"I can't decide if that's crazy or exciting!"

Constance laughed. "I think it's a little of both."

Mary nodded. "Perhaps. We're going to miss having you here. But I'm a little excited I can move into a larger bedroom." She stopped walking. "You don't think Ma will let Johnny have it, do you?"

"No, I think you'll get it if you want it. You'll be the eldest at home."

"I guess that means I'll also have more chores."

"Probably."

"Then I'll miss you and be glad you're gone all at once."

"That seems fair to me."

Chapter Two

Leonard paced back and forth in front of the train depot, waiting for his bride. He knew so little about her, but the matchmaker had assured him she was the woman he needed. Finally, the train pulled into the station. It was on time, but he'd been fifteen minutes early, so it felt like it was late.

As he watched, people exited the train. Sioux Falls was just a whistle stop for the trains, so only a few people got off. An older couple who was obviously together. A woman with three small children. And a woman on her own. He prayed the woman coming for him was on her own and wasn't the one with three children. While he loved children, he wanted to have his own.

The woman with children walked to a man who embraced her, and he breathed a sigh of relief, walking to the woman who was traveling alone. "Are you Constance?"

She nodded. "And you must be Leonard."

"Yes! I was hoping that was you."

"I'm happy to not be standing at this station for hours waiting for a stranger." She grinned at him. "Now what?"

"The pastor is at the church waiting for us."

"All right. We're going to the church then." She smoothed her dress, wishing she had time to bathe, but she understood why she didn't.

"And we must be quick. I need to be at work in two hours, and that means getting married and getting you home first."

"All right. Shouldn't be too terribly hard to get what we need to do done. What hours do you work?"

"I work from four to midnight." He eyed her as if he was worried she wouldn't like him working those hours.

"Sounds perfect. I'll have supper waiting for you at home when you arrive, but only if there's food in the house. I can't magic something up with no supplies."

He laughed. "There's food. I had my friend's wife come over and make a list of everything a wife would need, and then I bought it all."

"Well, I'll have to thank her when I meet her then."

"Do you have a trunk?" he asked, looking around.

"Yes, it's there," she said pointing to a small black trunk.

"I'll get that on the wagon, and we'll head to the church. I'm ready to be married."

She nodded. "As am I. It's been a long journey, and I'm ready to get on with our new life together." She realized she wasn't wearing the new dress she'd planned to wear for the wedding, but that was fine as long as Ma never found out. She'd wear it for her first Sunday in her new church.

Once they were on the road, it only took a couple of minutes to get to the church. He helped her down and took her hand, pulling her toward the church. "Pastor Abrams is the one doing the ceremony. He said he'd have two witnesses there for us."

Inside the church, she felt at peace. It was a small church, but that didn't matter to her one whit. She'd be married and that's what really mattered.

Pastor Abrams called out to him. "Leonard, you found your bride!"

Leonard grinned. "I did. She got off the train just like she was supposed to, so we're getting married."

"That'll be nice," the pastor said.

The ceremony was over quickly, and when Leonard was told to kiss his bride, he held nothing back, grabbing Constance by the waist and pulling her to him. He kissed her for all he was worth, and Constance was a bit startled by it all.

"Sorry to run out so fast," Leonard said, "but I need to get her home before I head to work." He shook the pastor's hand, and Constance was sure she saw a coin pass from one hand to the other. It pleased her to know her new husband was thoughtful.

Pastor Abrams smiled. "Have a good night at work! Welcome to our community, Constance!"

With that, they left the church and he helped her into the wagon. "I want to have a few minutes to show you around the house before I have to leave," he explained.

"Oh, that would be nice."

"I live here in town, which is nice for shopping and worship," he said. "The house isn't grand by any means, but it's comfortable. It has three bedrooms, and there's even a water closet. I think you'll be comfortable there."

"It sounds lovely. We didn't have a water closet back east."

"The winters are harsh here, so I put one in. I hate going outside in the middle of the night and freezing my bottom off."

Constance nodded, grinning. "I hated that back home."

"So, tell me about yourself and why you chose to answer the letter."

"My reason seems mostly shallow, but I hope you'll listen. I was born into a family of morning people. They're all up before the rooster crows, and I was never like that. I like to walk at midnight, and live the same pace as everyone else, and I get the same amount of sleep, but I'm in bed much later." She sighed. "My mother told me I was lazy a lot."

"It's not lazy!" He shook his head. "I like that you are a night owl like me. I drive for the freight company because I love to be awake at night. Most nights I'll be home by about quarter past midnight. Is that too late for you?"

"Not at all. I could easily stay up until three in the morning, but then I need to sleep until eleven."

"Sounds good to me. We'll get along great in that regard." He pulled up in front of a small house and helped her down. "This is my place. You're welcome to make any décor changes you'd like. I think it's decorated the way I do everything in life—haphazardly."

She grinned. "I'm sure there will be things I want to change to my taste. It'll all work out in the end."

He took her trunk and led her toward the house, opening the door wide to allow her to enter first. He'd paid a lady to come in and clean for him, so Constance wouldn't be disgusted by the state of things.

She stopped in the entryway of the house, seeing the kitchen straight ahead and the parlor to her left. Unsure of which way to go, Constance stood in the middle of the room, feeling like she was invading Leonard's privacy.

Leonard set the trunk down and put a hand on her shoulder. "This is your home now. Go where you want."

Constance chose to go into the kitchen first. There were cabinets everywhere, which thrilled her. She could keep the kitchen clean with so much space to store food and dishes. "Is there a cellar for food as well?" she asked.

He nodded. "I have potatoes, carrots, and all the food my mother canned for me down there. She's certain I'll starve to death if she doesn't provide me with food from her garden." He shook his head.

"Sounds like she loves you. You can't complain about that. Is she nearby?"

"Yes, I grew up on a farm outside town. My parents both still live there."

"I look forward to meeting them." Truthfully, she was nervous about it, but that was normal as far as she was concerned.

"They attend the church we were married in, so you'll meet them on Sunday." He walked through the kitchen into the bedroom. "This is the room we'll share. There are two other bedrooms upstairs that you can explore later. I just want you to see the basics before I head out to work for the night."

She frowned. "I won't have time to make a real meal before you go!"

"That's all right. My friend's wife brought over a big pot of chicken and dumplings for us to warm and eat today. You don't have to start cooking until tomorrow if that's your preference. You must be tired after a week on the train."

She smiled. "We'll see how that works out. I'll try to cook if I can force myself to do it."

He chuckled. "But if you could heat up the chicken and dumplings…"

"I'd be happy to." She went to his ice box, saying a silent prayer of thanks that he had the modern appliance, and pulled out the soup he'd mentioned. Starting the stove, she put the pot in the middle of the stove where it would get the most heat. She'd have to constantly stir it, but at least it would heat up quickly.

While it warmed, she investigated the bedroom she'd share with Leonard, noting that he'd placed her trunk at the foot of the bed. It seemed odd to think she'd be sharing a bed with a stranger, but with Leonard, it didn't feel unnatural.

She set the table in between stirring the food, and when it was ready, she served up two big bowls of the chicken dish. "I hope you're hungry!"

He nodded. "Starving. I usually eat a little earlier in the day. I take a meal to work with me, and then I eat when I get home. I hope that won't be too strange for you."

She shook her head. "I'm nothing if not flexible."

After a short prayer of thanks, they dug into the meal, and Constance was pleased to realize her chicken and dumplings were much better than the ones she was eating. These weren't bad, but she really preferred her own. It was good to realize that.

After the meal, he gave her a quick peck on the cheek and disappeared out the door. She did the dishes and unpacked her things, looking in the ice box for something she could serve for supper. She felt as if she was auditioning for the part of wife, and she wanted to start off on the right foot, not serving something some other woman had made.

There was a chicken in the ice box, and she pulled it out, planning to make fried chicken with mashed potatoes and a cream gravy to go with it. Surely, he would be happy with her serving something so delicious.

She glanced at the clock, seeing that it was only four in the afternoon, and she didn't have to have supper ready until midnight. So, she put the chicken back into the ice box and looked around for some cleaning that needed to be done, but everything was spotless. Why did the man need a wife if not to clean for him? She had no idea, but she'd look around and find something to do.

After a short while of exploring the house, she yawned and realized the perfect answer was for her to take a nap so she could stay awake until midnight. There was no way to sleep late on a train, so she had been up early every day since leaving Beckham.

She took a nice long nap, and then settled herself at the table with paper, pen, and ink to write a letter home and let everyone know she'd arrived safely.

Her letter to her mother was short and sweet, explaining she'd arrived safely and was now married and settling into her new house. Then she wrote a second letter to Elizabeth Tandy, telling her the same thing. She was thankful that Elizabeth had sent her to South Dakota. It seemed like it would be a pleasant place for her to live.

She still had a few hours before Leonard was to arrive home, so she went from room to room, thinking about the changes she wanted to make. She wanted red and white gingham curtains and a matching tablecloth for the kitchen. Hopefully Leonard wouldn't mind if she bought the supplies the following day. She would make herself crazy without work to do.

She made a list of the things that needed to be refreshed, and then she went into the kitchen to cook supper. It would be ready early, but that couldn't be a bad thing. There was no bread anywhere, so she mixed up a batch and set it out to rise before she mixed the breading for the chicken.

She peeled a small mound of potatoes to eat with the chicken and once they were on to boil, she punched down the bread. Thirty minutes before she expected Leonard, she put the bread in the oven and fried the chicken. It was her first meal to cook as a married woman, and she wanted it to be just perfect.

She even had most of the dishes from the meal done when Leonard walked in the door, tired from his hard day at work. She fixed their plates while he washed his hands, and they sat together to eat. "I hope you like fried chicken."

"Of course, I do!" he said. "And this smells delicious."

They held hands during their prayer, and then they both dug into the food she'd prepared. "I think there should be enough for your meal at work tomorrow," she said softly.

"I'm just thrilled you made fresh bread. I buy bread from the bakery, but it's just not the same as smelling it as you walk into your house."

She smiled, nodding. "I agree. I love baked goods, so I hope you don't mind eating them a lot."

"You will not hear me complain." He finished off his mashed potatoes and reached for more. "This gravy is wonderful."

"It's what my mother always made with fried chicken, so she taught me to do the same."

Leonard smiled. "I'll have to thank her when we meet."

"She'd be pleased. Oh, I wrote a couple of letters and need to post them tomorrow."

"Easy enough. I'll take you to the mercantile, and you can mail them from there."

"I'd like that," she said. "Could I also get a bit of fabric while we're out?"

"Do you need a new dress?" he asked.

She shook her head. "No, but I would like curtains for the kitchen and parlor, and a tablecloth and some pillows. Just things to make the house my own."

He grinned. "I had a feeling you'd enjoy changing things."

Constance shrugged. "Everything is beautiful the way it is, but it just doesn't feel homey."

"Oh, I agree. My mother offered to sew for me, but I wanted that to be left up to my wife whenever I married."

"You asked why I agreed to be a mail-order bride. Why did you send for one?" she asked.

"Because I have a hard time meeting women with the strange hours I keep. The only women in church are already married, and it just felt like the smart way to go about things."

"I see. Well, whatever reason, I'm glad I was the one who ended up with your letter. I think we're going to be very happy together."

"I sure hope so." He pushed away from the table. "I'll be in the parlor when you're finished with the dishes."

Constance watched him go with a smile. She was glad he wasn't meddling with her work.

Chapter Three

As Constance finished the dishes, she couldn't help but wonder if Leonard was going to expect her to consummate the marriage that night. She wasn't certain she was ready, and hopefully he wasn't ready either. Wouldn't it be better if they got to know one another and learned all they could before they married?

When she joined him in the parlor, she planned to bring up the idea of waiting with him, but she found him all sprawled out, reading from the Bible, and he looked very sweet that way. She was pleased to find herself married to a Christian man.

"Dishes are finished," she said, taking the seat beside him on the sofa. "Do you usually stay up for a while, or do you go to bed after you've eaten?"

"I'm usually up for another hour or two. Does that bother you?"

She laughed softly. "I was hoping you'd say that. I do enjoy being up at night. I love to walk and look at the stars."

He smiled. "Let's go."

"Really? You wouldn't mind?"

"Not at all. Did you live in the city back east or in the country?" he asked.

"Country. My father was a farmer just outside of Beckham, Massachusetts, which is where the matchmaker you wrote your letter to lives."

"I see. And did you enjoy being a farmer's daughter?" he asked.

"All except for the early mornings," she said with a grin.

"The earliest morning we'll have is for church on Sundays, and the service is at eleven, so we won't really have to be up before ten."

"That sounds like it won't be a problem," she said, pulling on her coat and hat. It was spring, but it was still cold in the middle of the night.

Leonard pulled on a coat as well, and they left the house, walking down a quiet street, hand-in-hand. "I really love Sioux Falls," he said. "It's a bustling town since the railroad came, but it's still small enough to feel like home."

"That's really nice. Beckham was the same. Big enough to have what we needed, but small enough that we could be happy there. I didn't know everyone, but I didn't have to. I knew the people who mattered to me."

He nodded emphatically. "That's how it is for me here. I do hope you're going to love Sioux Falls as much as I do."

"I'm sure I will. It's nice to know my mother isn't going to tell me what to do and when to wake up. She'd be angry every time I slept through the rooster's crowing...so most days." She grinned at him. "I really feel like I thrive at night."

"I always have as well. My pa thought I was the laziest human alive because I slept until it was time for breakfast. He thought I should be up seeing to the livestock before the sun was up."

"It sounds like we need each other, if only to be around people who are on the same schedule we are!" She smiled. "Just promise me our children won't be forced to adhere to our schedule, and they'll be allowed to love mornings if they choose to."

"Oh, absolutely. I don't mind being awake when others are asleep. The world is too precious to only see when it's crowded. I hope my child will understand that, but if he or she loves mornings, I won't say a word."

"How many children do you want?" Constance asked.

"I don't know...four or five? You?"

"Sounds good to me. There were three in my family."

"I have six brothers. I'm the youngest."

"I'm the oldest," she said with a smile. "Did you like being the youngest?"

"I probably would have enjoyed it more if my brothers hadn't constantly teased me, but it's okay. They're all farmers now, and I'm doing something I love." Leonard turned onto another street to loop back around to their house.

"You don't think they love farming?" she asked.

"I honestly have no idea. They always seemed like the type to do whatever was expected of them. They were expected to be up early, so they were. They were expected to farm like Pa, so they did." He shrugged. "I didn't do anything expected of me, I'm afraid."

"I will just be careful to have no expectations. Well, other than not drinking or..."

"Or cheating? How about I just promise not to break the ten commandments, and we'll all be content."

"That works for me." Staring straight ahead, she asked the question on her mind. "Do you expect to consummate the marriage tonight?"

"No, I really don't. I figured we'd take our time getting to know one another before we jump into that."

"How much time are you thinking?" she asked.

"I have no idea. Maybe tomorrow, but maybe not for a month or two. We'll see how it goes."

"All right." Constance would have preferred a date to mark on her calendar, so she knew what was expected, but that was all right. At least he was being kind about waiting.

"Supper was wonderful tonight. You must have experience cooking."

"From the time I was twelve, my mother expected me to make supper for the family twice per week. She'd been teaching me up until that point, but that's when she declared I was old enough to plan, shop for, and make a meal. I've always enjoyed cooking."

"Good. I really enjoy eating."

She laughed. "I will probably bake a cake tomorrow. Is there anything in particular you'd like me to make for our midnight meal?" Oh, how she loved knowing midnight would be part of her day.

"Hmm...I'm awfully partial to roast."

"Then I'll see to that. I didn't notice one in your ice box, but if there's a butcher nearby, I'd be happy to buy one for us."

"There is. I'll give you a quick walking tour tomorrow so you can learn where everything is. We live in a good spot because it's easy to walk to church, the mercantile, and the butcher shop. You won't need to wait on me to drive you places."

"I can hitch up horses and drive," she said softly. "I've been doing it my entire life."

"I think it's great you know how, but hopefully you won't need to." He turned to walk up to their house. "I'm glad you're here, Constance."

"I'm really happy to be here."

He gave her time to get ready for bed, and she put on her nightgown and climbed between the sheets. She was tired, but it was a good tired.

When Leonard joined her, he sat down on the edge of the bed and removed his clothes before sliding into bed. He obviously didn't wear a nightshirt as her pa always had. Reaching out to her, he pulled her close, kissing her forehead gently. "Sleep, and we'll have another busy day tomorrow," he told her.

Constance snuggled close to her new husband. She'd never slept with another person, so it was strange, but she had a feeling she would like sleeping with him. There was just something about the man that made her feel safe and at home.

Who would have thought moving across the country to marry a stranger could possibly be the right thing to do? But for her it had been. She only hoped he felt the same way about her.

*****

When Constance woke in the morning, it was to find Leonard had all the covers on the other side of the bed, while she lay shivering. Shaking her head, she got dressed and went into the kitchen to fix breakfast. It was past eleven, which was the latest she'd ever been allowed to sleep. Even when she'd been ill, her mother had thought she should be up before nine.

It felt good to sleep as late as she had. She made a quick breakfast, realizing she would probably be making four meals per day. That was all right though. As long as they were small meals it should all be fine.

She'd just taken the bacon up from the skillet when Leonard came out of the bedroom. "Did you put all the covers on me when you got up?" he asked, looking confused.

"No, I spent the night shivering while you stole the covers. You'd think you'd have better manners than that," she joked.

"I'll try to leave you some tonight." He dropped a kiss to her nose. "What are you making?"

"Bacon, eggs, and toast. I hope that's all right."

"Sure. I like my eggs scrambled."

"Then I'll make them all that way." She cracked six eggs into the skillet and added a dash of milk, immediately mixing them so they would be the desired consistency. "Are you still taking me for a tour this morning?"

"I'd love to," he told her. It was exciting for him to finally have her there. They would be able to explore together, and he could already see she loved the idea.

After breakfast, he took her first to the mercantile, where she mailed the letter and chose the fabrics she wanted for the kitchen and parlor. She'd have to redo the bedroom eventually, but as she'd be asleep in there more than she'd be awake, the other rooms took precedence in her mind.

He purchased the fabric, letting the merchant know that she could always charge to his account, and the two of them left for the butcher shop. Constance chose a large piece of meat, knowing she'd make some for supper, and she could make a stew out of it the following night. She was well versed in using every last bit of meat.

"Do you hunt?" she asked Leonard as they were leaving the butcher. She could make meat last longer if he brought her fresh meat that way.

He shook his head. "I never really enjoyed hunting as a boy, so I stopped as soon as I moved out of my father's house. My brothers will sometimes share the meat they kill with me, so I have a steady supply of meat, even without the butcher shop."

"Oh, good. I want to stretch every penny as far as I can."

He chuckled. "I'd like that a lot, but don't go overboard. I make a good wage, and I don't need you to hurt yourself trying to save money."

"I'll do my best," she said with a smile. "Today I'll be occupied with sewing all day. I'm excited, though sewing dresses is not something I'm fond of. I prefer to do the easy sewing projects like curtains and pillows."

"Well, I won't show you my mending basket for a few days then."

"You have a mending basket?" she asked, surprised.

"Yes. My ma usually takes it home once a month or so, but she'll expect you to do it now."

"That won't bother me a bit. I'll enjoy working on your mending."

"How do you know that if you don't like sewing?" Leonard asked.

Constance shrugged. "Because I know I like you, and I want to do things for you. Beyond cooking, which I already enjoy."

"I hope you're right. It would be nice." He carried her shopping basket home, and she put the meat into the ice box so she could cook it when it was time. "Let's sit together for a while before I have to leave."

She nodded. "All right." He pulled her toward the parlor, and she was happy to sit beside him on the sofa. "Did you want to talk about something?"

"No, I just thought I'd enjoy kissing you a bit before I have to leave for work."

"I'd like that," she said, surprising herself. She had never really been kissed before Leonard, and she was truly astonished at how much she enjoyed kissing him.

He lowered his head, capturing her lips with his, a hand going to the nape of her neck to cradle the back of her head. Deepening the kiss, he used his tongue to touch hers, once again startling Constance.

"I don't know if touching tongues is allowed…"

He chuckled. "We're married. Everything is allowed now."

Moving closer to him, she said, "Okay, do it again then!"

They sat there together for a long while, kissing and getting to know one another's bodies. When his hand cupped her breast through her dress, she gasped in surprise. "Is that all right? You're certain?"

He nodded emphatically. "I'm positive. God made women beautiful so men could enjoy them…after they're married of course."

"Oh, of course." She looked at him. "Does that mean I can touch your chest? Is that allowed?"

He smiled. "Do you want to touch me there?"

"I want to touch you everywhere!" she said.

"I have a feeling we're not going to wait terribly long to go to bed together," he told her.

"We slept together last night."

"I mean before we consummate the marriage, and I think you knew exactly what I meant, didn't you?"

She laughed, nodding. "I wouldn't object if you wanted to consummate."

He took a deep breath. "Tonight then. We'll skip the walk and exercise a different way."

Leaning toward him she kissed him once more. "I need to fix your meal before you leave for work. Do you want the chicken and dumplings again or the fried chicken?" She'd already made up his lunch pail with bacon sandwiches from their breakfast that morning.

"Fried chicken," he told her. "And I hope there are mashed potatoes and gravy left!"

"There's enough of everything. I'll need to bake some more bread today, now that I have an idea of how much you'll eat. I want to keep you satisfied."

He nodded. "I have a feeling you will."

Before leaving for work a short while later, he once again kissed her passionately. "I'm going to think about you all day."

"I hope so. I like when you think about me," she said, watching as he walked away until he was out of sight. Then she did the dishes and thought about the idea of consummating their marriage. As a farm girl, she knew the mechanics of the marriage act, but the cows had never seemed pleased when they were mounted by the bulls. Hopefully it wouldn't be as bad as it was for cows.

Her married friends had told her it was wonderful though, and she was going to cling to that thought all day. It couldn't be all bad if her friends said they enjoyed it, could it?

It didn't make sense to wonder and fret about it she finally decided. She'd find out for herself in a few short hours, and then she would know for certain.

As she worked on the pillows for the parlor, she thought only of Leonard. Who would have thought she could start falling in love on her first full day in South Dakota?

Chapter Four

Constance had finished the curtains for the kitchen and the tablecloth by the time Leonard was home from work. And there was a pot roast ready to come out of the oven. As soon as she heard the door open, she pulled out the pot roast and added some of the liquid from it to a pot, mixing in the water and flour she'd already mixed together.

It took less than five minutes to get supper on the table. Leonard nodded at the tablecloth. "This is nice. And I really like the curtains!"

Constance carried their plates to the small table. "I do too. This is just what I'd pictured when I said I wanted to do it as well. Some of my projects don't turn out exactly as I want them, but this one did."

"I think it looks wonderful," he told her.

She set their plates on the table and then sat down with him. "I'm glad you like it as much as I do. How was work tonight?"

"It was good. Busy as always. One of my favorite things about working the shift I do is I rarely have to deal with the owners of the stores. I've heard that's an absolute nightmare. But I have a key and I just take everything inside and leave it. Much better than it could be."

"Where all do you go at night?" she asked, fascinated by his work.

"I go to small cities around Sioux Falls, different ones each night. I have four stores on Mondays, five on Tuesdays, three on Wednesdays...That sort of thing."

"I see. Do you like what you do?"

"I really do. It gives me time to think about anything I want as I'm driving. Sometimes I like to make up stories in my head as I go from store to store. It's very cathartic for me."

"I'd probably like that as well. That's what I do when I walk at night. I think about different things or make up stories in my head. My mother thinks it means that there's something a bit off about me, but I don't care. I love walking and thinking more than I can express." She took her first bite of pot roast, thrilled with how it came out.

"This is delicious," he said. "Best pot roast I've ever eaten."

"I'm so glad you like it. My mother would never allow me to add onions to it because she doesn't care for them. I added all the onions I wanted, and I think it turned out much better."

Leonard nodded emphatically. "It's very good."

"Are there any foods you don't like that I should avoid making?"

He shrugged. "Lutefisk, blood sausage, and porridge." He answered quickly, so she knew he *really* didn't like those things.

"I will avoid all three. Are you good with bacon and eggs most mornings? I could do pancakes or johnny cakes or even French toast if you preferred."

"Just switch things around when you want to. I like eggs prepared just about any way, though scrambled are my favorite. I'm quite easy to please with food. Ma always called me her slop eater. If I wouldn't eat something, it automatically went to the pigs, but Ma would always try me first."

"I really am excited to meet your ma," she said.

"She'll like you. She considers all her daughters-in-law daughters of her heart. She was always sad she could only have boys."

"Are all your brothers married?" Constance asked.

Leonard nodded. "Yup. I'm the last. All of them have children as well."

"Are they much older?" she asked.

"The next youngest is five years older than me."

"It makes sense that they're all married with children then."

"Yes, it makes a lot of sense." He took another bite of the roast. "I want you to cook for me every day for the rest of my life."

"Isn't that what I agreed to yesterday afternoon?" she asked with a smile.

He tilted his head to one side for a moment, studying her. "You're like me. You think of a day as sleep to sleep. Not changing new days even when it's after midnight."

"That's true. How could I think any other way?" she asked.

All through dinner, though their conversation was lively, all she could think about was the night to come. It made sense for her to be nervous about consummating the marriage, but she wasn't sure she should be quite as nervous as she was.

After supper, he went into the parlor with a newspaper, and she cleaned the dishes, taking her time so as not to hurry things along. She never should have told him she was ready. She'd just gotten carried away in the moment, loving the kisses they shared.

Once she'd put the last dish away, there was no more putting off the inevitable moment, and she joined him in the parlor. "Dishes are done," she announced.

He set his paper down and patted the spot on the sofa beside him. "Join me."

She took a deep breath and did as he asked. Snuggling up to his side. When he turned and kissed her right away, she did her best not to think about what was about to happen and instead lost herself in his touch.

He cupped her face in his hands as his mouth explored hers. At first, she kept her hands folded in her lap, afraid to really do anything that would spur him on and make him go any faster with their consummation. After a minute or two, she put her hands on his shoulders and felt his strength through the lightweight fabric of his shirt. When she touched him, he reached to unbutton the top few buttons of his shirt.

"I need your touch against my bare skin."

Constance didn't need to be told twice. She was aching to feel his muscles beneath her fingers. Never having seen a man shirtless in her short life, she was surprised to feel a light dusting of hair there, but she just kept stroking, determined to enjoy the moment.

Leonard's fingers went to the buttons at the back of her neck, releasing each one in turn. He let his hands roam over her shoulders and bare back, though he wanted to strip her and take her there on the sofa. He knew he needed to go slowly though. He'd talked to his brother Luke about Constance coming to marry him, and his brother had given him advice on how to take things slowly to make it better for his bride.

When he stopped kissing her and pulled his head up to look deeply into her eyes, they were both out of breath. He stroked one finger along the side of her cheek and down to her lips, which were red and swollen from his kisses. "Touching you is better than I ever dreamed it could be."

She couldn't help but smile, wondering if it was all right to admit to him that she was enjoying his touch and his kisses. Afraid it would make him think she was ready, she only smiled at him, kissing the finger that touched her lips.

Leonard was sure this night would kill him, but he'd promised his brother and himself that things wouldn't go quickly. Even if he needed them to.

He pushed the top of her dress from her shoulders, and then he removed his shirt. At least they could touch one another.

When his hand cupped her breast through only her petticoat, she gasped in surprise. She was certain it wasn't Christian for a woman to enjoy what her husband did to her as much as she was.

"Is that okay?" he asked.

Constance nodded. "It feels good. I just worry..."

"It's not wrong," he told her.

She bit her lip, not sure whether to believe him.

"Read the Song of Solomon while I'm working tomorrow evening. It's rarely taught in churches because it mentions enjoying one another's bodies. If God didn't want us to enjoy what we do together, why would he make it feel so good?"

Deciding to believe him until she knew otherwise, she nodded, and sank in for another quick kiss. Her fingertips danced over his body, not really trying to arouse him, but learning about his body.

Finally, after a long while of just letting her touch him, he got to his feet, and took her hand. "That's enough parlor play. We're going to the bedroom."

Being pulled along behind Leonard should have frightened Constance, but instead it made her feel powerful. This man was in a hurry to make love with her, which meant she'd done something right. It had to be a good thing that he desired her that much, didn't it?

When they reached the bedroom, he was all hands, getting her out of her dress. When it fell from her breasts, she put her hands up to shield them. She'd always felt that her breasts were too small, but she could see Leonard didn't think so.

"Don't cover yourself," he said, his voice deeper and huskier than usual. "You're perfect in every way."

Constance blushed, but her hands dropped to her sides as Leonard stared at her bare body.

Then he made short work of undressing himself, standing before her with nothing on. She blushed at her first sight of a naked man. She'd had no idea a man's...well his thing would be so large. She remembered her brother as a baby, and his was always small and soft. Leonard's was anything but.

He scooped her up in his arms as if she weighed nothing and dropped her on the bed, quickly following her down. His hands were everywhere, and she had no time to think anymore. It was all she could do to keep breathing.

Much later, they lay together on the bed, her head resting on his shoulder. "That was...odd," she said.

He chuckled. "It felt very natural and perfect to me. I'm sorry you found it odd."

She shrugged. "I'm not saying it was bad...just...strange. I didn't expect to feel any pleasure from you touching me, and I did. But I didn't expect it to hurt as much as it did either. I hope it doesn't hurt every time."

"My brother told me it's better for the woman after the first few times. I have no experience with lovemaking myself."

"You mean...that was your first time too?" For some reason, it made Constance feel better that she'd married a man who hadn't been a philanderer.

He grinned. "Of course, it was." Brushing his lips across hers, he sighed. "I could do that again every day of my life."

She blushed. "You know there are times when we won't be able to?"

"Of course. I'll survive. I'll just want to." He reached over and turned down the lamp, and she realized she didn't know when he had lit it. Before he got home, she knew it had been off, but when they'd gone in there after their time in the parlor, it was already lit. He must have sneaked in and done it while she washed the dishes.

She turned more toward him and felt closer to him than she ever had any human being in her life. Snuggling against him seemed the perfect way to sleep, and so she did.

*****

By Friday, Constance was ready to have her husband home for two whole days. Leonard had told her that he only worked five-day weeks, and she loved that idea. Her father had often worked seven days per week, breaking the Sabbath every single week. He'd had no choice if he'd wanted to support his family.

When Leonard arrived home from work on Friday, Constance felt there was a celebration in order. She'd baked bread and a cake, and cooked a thick, hearty stew for their supper.

"The workweek is over!" she said, rushing to him and raising her lips for his kiss. "Now we get two entire days together!"

He smiled. "We do at that. How would you feel about going to a social and dance at the church tomorrow evening? There will be some men with instruments, and we will eat as a congregation and then dance the night away. Do you like to dance?"

Constance nodded. "I love to dance. I went to all the dances back in Beckham." She didn't add that she was always the girl in the corner, leaning against the wall, and making sure it didn't fall down.

"Well then, we're going to have fun dancing tomorrow!"

"Will your family be there?"

He shrugged. "Sometimes my brothers bring their families, but my parents will stay at home."

"Could we do a picnic for lunch tomorrow? Would you mind?"

"I'd love to. I'll hitch up the buggy, and we'll take a nice long drive. We can picnic by the river if you'd like."

Constance clapped. "I would adore that!" She'd always been drawn to water, and her parents had taken her to the beach multiple times.

"Then we have our whole day planned. Sunday will just be church and a quiet day at home, if that's all right with you."

"Of course. I don't need to always be doing something fun. I can stay home and be happy here."

"A lot of times on Sunday, Ma will have the whole family over for Sunday dinner. I haven't heard if she's doing that this week, but I have a feeling she's going to insist. She'll want the entire family to meet you and get to know you."

"I would like that a lot. I have no friends here, so it would be nice if I could meet some of your sisters-in-law. I'd love to become friends with them."

"I'm thinking Ma will have us, but if not, you really are content to spend the day at home?"

She smiled, turning and walking toward the kitchen. "Of course I am."

As he ate her cooking, he watched her, thinking that God had sent him the only woman in the world who was perfect for him, and he was glad. She could cook, and she enjoyed his attentions. What more could a man ask for in a wife?

"What are you thinking?" she asked, realizing he'd been watching her.

"That you're a woman who can truly make me happy. I'm so thankful I sent that letter to the matchmaker in your town. My life will never be the same."

Chapter Five

Constance made them a picnic lunch as soon as she had finished the breakfast dishes the following day. There was no picnic basket, as she would have liked, so she put all their food into his lunch pail. It would work until she could talk him into buying her a picnic basket. Perhaps she could request it for Christmas.

He came in from hitching the horses to the buggy as she was walking toward the door with their food. "We need to be home in time for me to cook for the church supper," she told him.

He nodded. "We'll go now and come back when we've eaten. I want to show you the beautiful area we live in."

"I'd love that!"

After helping her into the buggy, he talked to her about the history of the Indians in the area and the early settlers of Sioux Falls. They drove along the river as he stopped to point out several things, and they had their picnic near the falls and the abandoned Queen Bee Mill. He told her the story of the mill that had cost so much to build and was only open for two years.

"We just didn't have enough power from the river or enough wheat needing to be ground," he said, shaking his head. "It's still beautiful though."

"It is. Why it's the tallest building I've seen!"

"Seven stories," he said. "I hear someone else is planning to make a go of it, but no one can seem to make it work."

"That's really sad. I hate when buildings that are that beautiful can't be used for their intended purpose." She smiled. "Wouldn't it be fun to buy a building like that just to raise your family in? I'd think I was living in a castle!"

He frowned for a moment. "Do you not find our house large enough?"

Constance immediately regretted her words. "Oh, no! That's not what I meant at all. I'm just having a little moment of daydreaming. I think our house is wonderful. Why, I haven't even been upstairs to see the other bedrooms yet. And there's a water closet! I don't know of a woman who could find a way to complain of a house with a water closet."

"Are you sure?" He wanted her to be happy, and if that meant working three jobs, then he'd do it.

"I'm positive. I love our home. I just always dream about what life could be."

"Just so you're content with your real life…"

"So content!" She covered his hand with hers. "You know I'm happy here. And with you." She blushed as she said the second part, and she knew he'd understand what she meant.

He leaned down and brushed his lips against hers. "And I'm happy with you…"

Another buggy stopped and people got down, bringing a picnic with them as well. The man looked at them for a moment before raising his hand in greeting. "Ho there, Berry!"

Leonard raised a hand. "Fredricks." He wasn't nearly as enthusiastic with his greeting as the other man had been.

"Who's the lady?" the man asked.

Leonard sighed, realizing they would probably have company for the rest of their picnic. "This is my wife, Constance. Constance, this is Freddie Fredricks and his sister, Agatha."

"It's nice to meet you both," Constance said softly.

Agatha skipped over and sank down on the quilt they were eating their picnic upon. "I haven't met you before."

Constance smiled. "I just moved here from Massachusetts."

"Oh, well Leonard never told me he was marrying someone from back east, and I think that's rather rude, as he knew I'd set my cap for him." Agatha pouted.

Constance blinked a couple of times. "Well, I had no idea. I hope we can be friends anyway."

Agatha shook her head. "Probably not. Now I'll have to find another man to set my cap for. I usually just throw my bonnet at whomever I've decided I want to marry, so he'll know."

Constance did her best to hide a smile. "You'll have to find another man who doesn't mind having bonnets thrown at him then."

"Oh, Leonard got mad at me for it. He told me that ladies didn't throw things at men." Agatha shrugged. "At least it got his attention. I'd been making cow's eyes at him for just ages, and he never seemed to notice."

"Well, maybe he was busy looking somewhere else while you were making eyes at him."

"Probably. We went to school together, you know. Me, and Freddie, and Leonard. Leonard was always the smartest in school, but Freddie was always the one who stood in the corner most. He held the school's record. Right, Freddie?"

Freddie nodded. "That's right. I don't think Leonard ever stood in the corner."

Leonard wasn't sure how to respond to that, so he simply said, "The corner was always full. I wasn't about to fight over the spot." His eyes met Constance's, and he could see how amused she was, so he decided to let the others stay.

"Tell me some stories about your school," Constance said.

"Oh, there are so many stories, I wouldn't know where to start," Freddie said.

"I do!" Agatha said. "Leonard didn't want to be a farmer like the other boys in school, and he wasn't afraid to tell people. Once he fell asleep during class, and though the corner was full, he did have to write, 'I will not sleep in class,' one hundred times on the blackboard during our lunch hour."

Constance smiled at Leonard, imagining him sleeping in class. "I fell asleep in class once too, but my seatmate noticed, and she woke me before the teacher could."

"That's good!" Agatha said. "We all saw Leonard sleeping, but we just laughed, and he got caught. Isn't that funny?"

By the time they were finished eating, Constance had heard many stories of Leonard's misadventures at school. Stories she would remember so she could tell their children.

As soon as they got home, Constance started chicken on to boil and then she mixed up the dough for dumplings. Leonard had yet to try her chicken and dumplings, and she was eager for him to do so. She also thought they would be an effective way to make a first impression at the church supper.

While she worked at making supper for the social, Leonard went into the parlor and fixed a small hole she'd spotted in the wall where she was certain mice would come in.

As they drove with their pot and Constance in her best dress that she was supposed to be married in, she told him she'd like a cat. "We always had barn cats at home, but Ma would bring them in the house if we had a mouse problem. I'd like to get one for the house, so we don't have to worry about borrowing one." Besides, she'd always wanted a pet.

He looked at her. "It's important to you?"

"It is. We'll let it go in and out, so it's not stuck inside all the time, but I would love to have a kitten."

"A kitten won't take care of mice. They have to be a little older."

"Well, the kitten will learn. Please, Leonard?"

He couldn't say no to her, even though he believed cats belonged outside and not indoors. "I guess that would be all right. I'll ask around to see if anyone has a litter."

Constance squealed. "Oh, thank you!"

He chuckled. "You are an easy wife to please."

"I try hard."

As soon as they got to the church, Leonard took the pot from her, and they walked to the church together. She smiled and waved at Pastor Abrams whose wife was beside him. She walked to the couple, waiting for an introduction. Pastor Abrams smiled. "This is my wife, Penelope Abrams. Penelope, this is Mrs. Berry. I'm afraid I don't remember your first name." The pastor looked embarrassed for a moment. "I'm good with faces, but I never remember names."

Constance nodded. "I have a great deal of trouble with names as well," she said. "My Christian name is Constance. It's nice to meet you Mrs. Abrams. I'm looking forward to church tomorrow and getting to know the ladies."

"We have a quilting circle every Tuesday afternoon if you'd like to join us. It starts at two and goes until we all have to get home to put supper on the table."

"That sounds lovely." Constance smiled. "I'll be there."

"You don't have to bring your own quilt. We always get together to work on the same quilt, and then when that's done, someone else will bring one for us to quilt. Sometimes we even sell them to raise money for missionaries."

"I can't wait to go and meet everyone."

"Have you quilted before?"

"Oh, yes. My mother taught me when I was a girl."

Mrs. Abrams smiled. "You still seem a girl to me, but I have four grandchildren, so I must seem ancient to you."

"Not at all," Constance said. She turned when she felt a hand on her shoulder. Leonard stood over her.

"Good evening, Mrs. Abrams. Pastor."

"Good to see you, Leonard," Mrs. Abrams said. "Congratulations on finding this sweet girl."

Leonard smiled. "I'll always be happy I did."

Pastor Abrams smiled. "You know, I always worry about weddings. You never know how a marriage will turn out. I prefer a good funeral any day. I know who that person is."

Constance laughed. "I can see why you'd say that."

Leonard took Constance's arm. "I want to introduce you to two of my brothers and their wives."

"Oh, yes, please. It was a pleasure chatting with you, Pastor, Mrs. Abrams." Constance turned and followed Leonard to a group of people who were laughing together. She was nervous to meet his kin, but she was happy not to meet them all at once.

Leonard put his arm around her shoulders. "Luke, Peter, this is my bride, Constance. Constance, my brothers Luke and Peter."

Constance smiled. "It's so nice to meet you."

Both men nodded. "You as well," one of the brothers said.

"Which one are you?" Constance asked. With as many brothers as he had, she wanted to be able to learn their names slowly. She really did find names difficult.

"I'm Luke. I'm the one Leonard came to for advice on marital things."

One of the women snorted, and Constance was immediately drawn to her. The sound was anything but ladylike, but Constance had enough trouble being ladylike, she didn't mind it a bit. "And you are?"

"Luke's wife, Caroline. And the thought he could give anyone marital advice is just a joke in my eyes." Caroline shook her head as her eyes teased her husband.

"You'll pay for that, wife!" Luke said.

"I'm Betty," the other woman said. "I'm Peter's wife, and Peter knows better than to try to give marital advice."

"Last time I tried, I slept on the floor of the barn for a week," Peter said.

"Was that when you gave me advice before I got married?" Luke asked.

Peter nodded. "I will never even try that again."

"I don't blame you!" Leonard said, laughing with his brothers.

"Where are you from?" Betty asked Constance.

"I'm from Beckham, Massachusetts, a small town an hour's train ride from Boston."

"Oh, Boston," Caroline said. "I've always wanted to go there. There's such rich history there."

"There is," Constance agreed.

"Don't you miss it?"

Constance shrugged. "I haven't been gone long enough to miss it yet. Maybe when Leonard and I have our first fight it will happen. I do miss my family, though."

The other women laughed, but she felt Leonard tense up beside her. Did he really think they could be married for years and never fight?

"Where are your children?" Constance asked, changing the subject before Leonard got too upset. She wasn't sure why the subject bothered him, but it obviously did.

"We left them with Ma Berry," Betty said. "That's what she likes all of her daughters-in-law to call her."

"Oh, that's nice. I'm sure she's happy to spend some time with her grandchildren."

The two women exchanged a look with one another that Constance made a mental note to ask about later.

Someone rang the church bell then, and they all gathered together for the pastor's prayer over their meal. It was the first prayer Constance had heard from him, and she found him a bit long-winded, but what pastor wasn't?

Constance and Betty stood in line for food, while Caroline went to help serve. Constance would have happily helped, but Betty shook her head. "This church does rotations. Ten women serve with each social, and this is not our time. I'm sure we'll be working next month."

"I see. I will happily take my turn." Looking behind her, Constance made certain the men were elsewhere. "What was the look you and Caroline gave each other when I said Ma Berry must enjoy her time with the grandchildren?"

Betty looked around as well before answering. "Ma Berry is a good woman. Really. But she's not the most nurturing woman I've ever met. She'll watch the children on rare occasions, but it can't be often, and no more than two families' worth of children at a time. She won't say anything when the men are around, but when it's just us ladies, she'll tell us she paid her dues, and it's our turn now."

"I see," Constance said, shaking her head. "But she doesn't want her sons to know she feels that way?"

"She doesn't. I've tried to talk to Peter about it, but he won't believe it, so there's no point trying. It may be different with Leonard's children, since he's her youngest, but I doubt it. Mostly, we sisters swap children. So, if someone wants to have a special day with just her husband, or just needs some time to think, one of us will watch ours and theirs."

"Oh, that's nice. I guess I should start watching all your children so I can have a turn without mine."

Betty laughed. "That's not a bad idea. All of ours are growing up, and it will be hard for you to swap like we do."

"I'll have to make friends with some other newly married women," Constance said, grinning.

By the time they got to the front of the line, all the chicken and dumplings were gone. "I wonder what that was," Betty said, looking at the empty pot.

"I made chicken and dumplings," Constance said.

"The men seem to have polished them off."

"Do the men always eat first?"

"Yes, of course. Isn't it that way back east?"

"Sometimes," Constance said. It did seem odd to her that every man had eaten before a single woman got a bite. It didn't matter to her much, but it was something to note.

"How do you feel about the strange hours Leonard works?" Betty asked. "I could never deal with those hours."

"I love them," Constance said. And it was true. She couldn't be happier.

Chapter Six

After the meal, the band tuned up their instruments, and the men and women came together. For some reason, the meal was separated between men and women, though Constance didn't really understand the reasoning.

As soon as Leonard joined Constance, he put his hand in the middle of her back, as if he was claiming her. When Constance looked around, she could see several of the men looked disappointed, which surprised her. No one had thought of her as any sort of prize back east, but here she was with several men interested. She said a quick prayer of thanks that she was already married and wouldn't have to choose between men. That wouldn't have been something she would have enjoyed.

When the first song's opening notes filled the air, Leonard held his hand out to Constance, and she smiled, nodding. Never having danced before, it was astonishing how very right it felt to be held in Leonard's arms and following his lead to the music.

"Are there dances like this often?" she asked.

He looked down into her glowing face and nodded. "At least once a month when the weather is good."

"Oh, so nothing in the winter?"

"Ma and Pa invite everyone over on Saturday nights during the winter months. We play cards or we dance. There's always something to do with a family as big as mine."

"What do the children do?"

He shrugged. "They play card games amongst themselves, and they dance when there's music. Ma has a few toys they play with, or they go upstairs to the bedrooms my brothers and I shared, and they play up there. There are so many of them they always have fun."

"That sounds lovely." Constance looked forward to winter nights with his family. It sounded like her life would be full of activities, and that pleased her. Once a week was enough to spend like that though. She preferred her quiet time with Leonard. The change of pace every week would be nice. "What about the other weeks during the summer?"

"My siblings will invite us over. It's usually just two families getting together though. I turned down most of the invitations because I felt so alone, but now that we're married, I'll happily accept."

"It'll be nice to have your family over as well," Constance said, thinking of the elaborate meals she could make.

The song was over, so they returned to Peter, Luke, and their wives. Betty grinned at Constance. "You looked like you were having so much fun!"

"I've never danced before," Constance admitted. "I had no idea how much fun it was to be on the dancefloor, instead of watching as I leaned against the wall."

Betty laughed. "I was a wallflower too." She elbowed Peter. "He never could get up the courage to ask me to dance, so I stood there, waiting for what seemed like forever."

"So how did you finally get together?"

"I asked him to dance. He refused but asked if he could take me for a walk the following evening." Betty shook her head. "He was afraid to dance in public until I taught him how much fun it can be."

Peter shook his head. "I'd had my eye on her for a long time. I guess I just wasn't sure how she felt about me, so I didn't ask."

"What about you?" Constance asked Caroline. "Did Luke ask you to dance?"

Caroline shook her head. "Luke told me he was going to marry me when we were ten. I told him he'd have to ask properly, so when we finished school, he came to me, dropped to one knee, and asked me to marry him. There was no real courting. We just always planned to marry."

"That's sweet," Constance said.

"I thought so." Caroline looked up at Luke, and the look was so loving, Constance almost felt as if she was intruding on a private moment.

Leonard shook his head. "Nah, the way we did it is more romantic. We agreed to marry sight unseen." He slipped his arm around her waist and kissed her cheek. "Our story is special to me in every way."

Constance smiled at him. She wasn't sure she agreed, but that was all right. She was happy with her marriage. How could she have any complaints when she was married to such a caring man?

After the dance, Leonard took Constance home. "You seem to have enjoyed yourself."

"I did! I'm glad I got to meet your sisters-in-law before everyone else in the family. I'm a little nervous about church tomorrow." Constance felt strange admitting it, but he couldn't help her if he didn't know how she felt.

"Oh, don't worry. My family is going to love you."

She looked at him for a moment in the light of the full moon, but then she shrugged. "I certainly hope so." What she really wanted though was his love. Not sure she'd ever get it, she'd have to settle for his family loving her.

For their midnight meal, she served the chicken and dumplings she'd reserved from her contribution to the church social. She wasn't sure if he'd eaten it at the gathering, but she wanted him to try it, so he could see she was a superior cook to his friend's wife.

Leonard frowned at his plate. "I've had a lot of chicken and dumplings meals this week."

"But they were all made by your friend's wife. This was made by me." Tears sprang to her eyes, but she blinked them away. Constance felt chastised for cooking her favorite meal for him, and it stung a bit.

"I guess." He stuck his spoon into the food. "I'll survive it." He took a bite and nodded. "This is really good." He could tell he'd upset her, and he wanted to make it better, but he didn't know how. "Best chicken and dumplings I've ever had."

"But you don't like chicken and dumplings?" she asked.

"They're not my favorite. I really am a man who loves his beef."

"I'll try to do better in the future," she said, her voice sounding a little off, even to her own years.

"We've only been married five days. You can't know everything about me."

"I would if we'd courted like a normal couple." Constance had already felt like her marriage to Leonard was inferior, but his not liking chicken and dumplings made it even worse.

"We are a normal couple," he said, covering her hand with his. "Just because we met differently than my brothers met their wives, I don't think our marriage is any less than theirs."

She nodded but didn't meet his eyes. She felt as if all her hopes and dreams had been squashed by his words. Maybe she wasn't going to live happily ever after no matter what her fantasies had been about this marriage.

*****

Constance was still feeling a bit less the following morning. They were up earlier than they usually were so they could be on time for church, and Leonard didn't seem to realize anything was even wrong. That was good, she guessed. That way he wouldn't try to fix something or pretend to feel something he didn't.

On their way to church, he talked about all of his brothers. "Amos is the oldest, then comes Peter, Jack, Stan, Charles, and Luke. All are married. All have at least three children, sometimes four. And then Amos has five."

She nodded. "That's a big family."

"It is, but it's a fun one. I'm so excited about you meeting my ma."

"Betty and Caroline said I should call her Ma Berry."

"Yes, that's what she has all her daughters-in-law call her. That way there's no confusion when the women mention Ma."

Constance smiled. "I think it's a good way to do things."

Leonard parked the wagon on the church lawn and helped Constance to her feet. "If I wasn't expecting an invitation for Sunday dinner from Ma, we would have walked. It's a beautiful morning."

"Yes, it is. I think I'm going to like your South Dakota."

He offered her his arm, and she took it. They walked into the church together, his eyes scanning the small crowd there. "There she is." He walked toward one side of the church and stopped in front of an older woman. "Ma, this is my wife, Constance. Constance, this is my ma." He had a huge grin on his face as he introduced the two of them, excited they were finally meeting.

Mrs. Berry looked Constance up and down. "You look too skinny to have babies." She put her hands out and grabbed Constance's hips. "Maybe you can do it." Looking at her son, she said, "Don't get too attached to this one. You may need to have someone waiting for you after she dies in childbirth."

Constance was horrified by the words, wondering what her new mother-in-law was thinking to say that. "I'm built like my mother, and she's had three children with no problem."

"Time will tell, won't it?"

Constance looked behind her for Leonard, trying to see if he'd stand up for her, but to her amazement, he was across the church, talking to some men. "It's a pleasure to meet you finally, Mrs. Berry."

A grunt was the response she got. Constance longed for something to say to the woman, but no words were forthcoming.

Two minutes went by that way, seeming like forever. And then Betty and Caroline were on either side of Constance, Betty saying brightly, "Good morning, Ma Berry. I see you've met our Constance."

Mrs. Berry nodded. "I did."

"Isn't she lovely?" Caroline asked.

"I suppose you'd call her that," Mrs. Berry said. She looked down her nose at the three women in front of her.

Betty took Caroline's arm. "Is it all right if I introduce her around? I'm sure everyone is dying to meet her!"

"I suppose that's fine."

With that, Betty pulled Constance away from their mother-in-law. "You okay?" Betty whispered.

Constance nodded. "I think so."

"She measures all of our hips the same way, and she always announces we'll die in childbirth," Caroline said. "It seems to be a rite of passage."

"I think it's awful!" Constance said. "I felt like a slab of meat."

"We all did," Caroline said soothingly. "I'd known the family my entire life and she still did that to me. If I hadn't been so in love with Luke, I would never have married him."

"Oh. I had no idea!"

Betty nodded. "She's just...odd. We all deal with it. But don't worry...the support you get from your sisters-in-law will make up for how she is." Betty stopped walking in front of a small group of women. "And here they are!"

One by one, Betty and Caroline introduced Constance to her new sisters-in-law. As she was greeted by each of them, she felt welcomed in a way she certainly hadn't with Mrs. Berry.

"Are you and Leonard going to Ma Berry's for Sunday dinner?" Patsy, Amos's wife, asked.

"I think we are," Constance said, trying not to let it show on her face she didn't want to go. She needed to not make waves.

"We'll all get to know one another better there," Sally, Jack's wife, said. "It'll all be fine."

None of the others mentioned what had just happened between Constance and their mother-in-law, but she saw understanding on each of their faces. It seemed that the sisters-in-law really would support her, and that was all she needed at that moment. Well, that and Leonard's love, but she had a feeling that would not be forthcoming.

During the service, Constance sat with Leonard, paying rapt attention to the sermon. Pastor Abrams had chosen loving thy neighbor as his theme that week, and it was definitely a favorite sermon topic.

As soon as the service was over, she got into the buggy with Leonard, and they drove out to his parents' farm. It was a longer drive than Constance expected, but it could be made in under thirty minutes.

"I don't think your ma likes me," Constance said after a few minutes of driving along in silence.

"Of course she does. Ma likes everyone."

Constance realized the man truly believed what he said. "I think she wants me to die in childbirth."

"There's no call for you to say things like that about my ma. Ever. I will never put up with it."

And that's when Constance realized she would be relying on her sisters-in-law much more than she'd ever realized she would. But she would do her best to make the most of the situation. She could put up with one bad apple in her new family in exchange for six sweet sisters.

At the house, Leonard set the brake and helped Constance down. "No bad talk about my ma. You hear me?" He was starting to think he'd made a mistake by marrying Constance. If she was going to say bad things about his mother, he didn't know what to do.

Once they were inside, Constance immediately asked if she could help with anything, and Mrs. Berry pointed to a hook where multiple aprons hung. Constance donned one before looking to her mother-in-law to see what she should do.

"You can peel the potatoes," Mrs. Berry said, and when Constance looked, she saw an entire mountain of potatoes ready to be peeled.

None of the others were there yet, so Constance went to the basin and began peeling, one potato after another.

Once the other sisters-in-law started to arrive, it felt as if the air thinned out a bit, and Constance wasn't strangling on the words she wanted to say to her mother-in-law.

One of the other women took a knife out and helped Constance with the potatoes. "I've forgotten your name," Constance said. "I'm sorry."

"I'm Judy. Charles is my husband."

"Thank you for making it clear how you fit into the family," Constance said. "It's hard to keep track of everyone."

"Oh, I know. It's a big family."

"What about your family?" Constance asked. "Is it as large?"

Judy shook her head. "No, I was an only child. My ma wanted a handful, but she died when I was three, and Pa never remarried. So it was just me and my pa. He's remarried now, which I think is good, but we spent a lot of years with just the two of us. I think he was relieved when Charles asked for my hand. It made it easier for him to move on with his life. He has three more children now."

"I think that's lovely. He must have really cared about you to remain alone for so long after your mother died."

Judy smiled. "He's a good father."

"I'm glad! So does he have children around the same age as yours?" Constance asked, thinking about how odd that would be.

"He does. My eldest is older than any of his three with his new wife. I have the youngest out of us though. My little girl is just eighteen months. Though his wife is with child again. It's amazing to me to see his happiness with Margaret."

"That's very sweet. I'm glad you have him in your life."

Judy nodded. "As am I. I have the Berrys of course, but it's not the same as having a family of my own."

Constance nodded. "I'm sure it's not. I miss my family something fierce."

Constance didn't notice Leonard behind her or his reaction to her words.

Chapter Seven

During the meal, Constance got to know her father-in-law a bit, finding him a jovial man. He seemed to be the exact antithesis of his wife, who seemed broody and negative. They were an odd pair, but they were happy with each other, both deferring to the other at different times.

Constance was quiet, listening to the chatter around her. The sisters were all planning to do different things and seeing who needed help. "I would love to have everyone over tomorrow afternoon," Judy said. "I think it would be nice if we all welcomed Constance with an afternoon tea."

The sisters all nodded enthusiastically. "I suppose I'm not invited," Mrs. Berry said, and Constance froze. She hoped the woman wouldn't want to join them, as she seemed to dislike everyone so much.

"Of course, you're invited, Ma Berry. Would you like to bring one of your cakes for our dessert?"

"I think it would be better if we all learned what Constance's cooking is like. Constance, you bring the cake."

"Yes, ma'am," Constance said, not wanting to cause any tension. "I enjoy baking."

Mrs. Berry let her eyes rest on her newest—and youngest—daughter-in-law. "Well, then you may bake for all of us."

"I'll have to bring my two little ones," Caroline said. "They're not in school yet." She gave Constance a sympathetic glance.

"Where are the children?" Constance asked, only then realizing the children weren't seated with them.

"The men make them a huge table out of two sawhorses and some sheets of wood. They can be messy while they eat, and there's no mess to clean up. Old Rebel cleans it up for them," Betty said. "It's a good arrangement."

Mrs. Berry snorted. "Anything that keeps food off my floors is a good arrangement." She looked at Constance. "If you drop any food, know that you will be sweeping it up yourself."

"Yes, ma'am," Constance said. What other words were there? She couldn't believe Leonard couldn't see how his mother was treating her—and apparently all of her other daughters-in-law as well.

Everyone pretended that nothing untoward was said, but it obviously made the other sisters as uncomfortable as it made Constance. The men must be so used to the way Mrs. Berry said things that no one took offense.

After the meal, Constance volunteered to sweep. She hadn't dropped any food, but she was willing to do her part in keeping the old woman happy. Surely she would be happier once her house was clean again.

With all seven daughters-in-law working to clean the kitchen, there was nothing for Ma Berry to do but sit and watch, and she seemed to like it that way. Looking around the house, Constance noticed it was absolutely immaculate. Even though children had been there the night before. Surely her mother-in-law hadn't locked them in a room by themselves so they couldn't mess anything.

After the meal, there was a bit of visiting, and then everyone was loading into buggies and wagons and heading home. "How far from here do you live?" Constance asked Judy as they were walking to their respective conveyances.

"The next farm over is ours. All of us live in a big clump here. All except you and Leonard." Judy leaned close. "Just be happy Leonard had moved away from everyone else before you married, because you'd definitely be blamed for his absence otherwise!"

Constance grinned. "It's good to feel like I'm not all alone in this."

"You are not at all. Any one of us would be there for you if you only asked. Just keep in mind we've all been there. It's not you. It's her."

"Thank you." Constance hugged Judy before turning and getting into the buggy with Leonard. She couldn't help but notice that he was already on the seat with the leads in his hands, and he had no intention of helping her up.

After climbing into the buggy on her own, Constance covered herself with the lap robe. She had no desire to get her new dress dirty. No, it would stay as clean as it had been when she'd first donned it.

As they drove away from the house, Leonard asked, "Why did you say that about Ma on the way here?"

"She told me I was too small to birth children. That's all. I guess I just took it the wrong way."

"You don't believe it anymore then?"

Not wanting to lie to her husband, Constance shrugged. "She seems to like me as much as all of your sisters-in-law."

He chuckled at that. "Well, maybe not as much as the others yet. You haven't given her a grandbaby."

Constance smiled and nodded. What else could she do? She didn't want to cause problems with her husband, even if his mother wasn't the kindest person she'd ever met. "What will we do for the rest of the day?" she asked.

"I don't know about you, but I was up much too early. I'm going to take a nap."

She smiled. "I do believe I'll join you." He was her husband and she was going to do all she could to make their marriage a happy one. Even if it meant that she would have to put up with his mother.

*****

The evening went well, with the two of them reading together in the parlor after their supper. Constance was very aware of Leonard watching her in a way he hadn't before that day, and she wasn't certain why, but she wasn't willing to rock the boat enough to ask.

"Do you miss your family?" he asked out of the blue.

She nodded. "Of course, I do. They're the people I've been with every day of my life. How could I not miss them?"

"You have a new family now." His words were quiet but spoken authoritatively.

"I do. But I can still love and miss my old family." Why couldn't he understand that her family was important to her just the same as his family was important to him?

"I guess I just never thought about you missing family from back east. I thought you'd come here, and mostly forget about them, and just be part of my family."

She blinked at him, astonished by his words. "Would you forget your family if you moved to the east?"

"Of course not. But that's different."

"Why is it different?" She really didn't understand him. She'd thought they were a great fit, and now it seemed like he was turning into someone else entirely—someone who had no empathy for her situation at all.

"Well, because you're a woman. You're supposed to leave your family and join your husband's. Why do you think you take on his family name and give up your own?"

"Do you really think that's why?" she asked, getting annoyed with him. But she had to keep calm. She couldn't let her temper show this early in the marriage, or he'd put her on a train right back to Massachusetts.

"Makes sense to me."

"Well, I'm sorry I can't give up missing my family as quickly as you think I should. I do wish I could sit down with my mother and discuss the events of the day. I've been writing her of course, but it's just not the same. A woman needs her mother."

"I think if you'd start thinking of my ma as your mother, you would miss yours less. She's a wonderful mother. You'll see."

Constance smiled and held her tongue. "I can see why you'd feel that way."

*****

Constance left for tea at Judy's house before Leonard left for work. As much as she'd wanted to be with him the week before, that's how much she wanted to ignore him. Spending every moment together had once sounded like a dream...now it sounded ridiculous. She was going to enjoy her time with her new sisters and ignore her new mother-in-law.

Leonard had given her directions out to his brother's home, and she went on horseback instead of worrying about taking a buggy. He'd wanted her to take a buggy, especially when she saddled the horse for herself. "I think you should take the buggy. There's no reason for you to ride around astride like a wild woman."

"There's also no reason not to. I'd walk to your brother's place if it wasn't so far. I promise, I can make it there and back without meeting an untimely demise." With that, she put her left foot in the stirrup and swung her right leg over the horse's back. "I'll have your midnight meal ready when you get home." She rode out of town with a cake in a makeshift contraption hanging from the saddle bag. It wasn't the best way to carry a cake, but it would certainly work.

It felt good to feel the wind on her face as she rode toward her destination. Her thoughts were her own for a bit, and she shook her head as she still seethed at Leonard's idea of her forgetting her own mother in favor of his.

When she reached the farmhouse, she dismounted, pulling the cake from the saddle bag and looking at it for a moment. The frosting had smudged a bit, but she could easily fix that once she was inside.

She'd made an angel food cake with a frosting she'd been making since she was a child. It was heavy on the lard, but she didn't think anyone would argue.

She knocked on the door, knowing she was there a bit earlier than everyone else. What did it matter? She had to fix the cake anyway.

Judy came to the door and opened it wide, inviting her in. "The children are down for a nap, so we have a minute or two to chat."

"I have to fix the cake first. The frosting smudged on the way."

Judy nodded, smiling. "You rode!"

"I did. And Leonard didn't like it one bit. He's very rigid in how he thinks things should be."

Judy nodded. "All of the men in this family are. They get it from their ma."

"How long should I expect to be under Mrs. Berry's intense scrutiny? She seems to hate me, but Leonard assures me she doesn't want me dead."

Judy laughed. "She doesn't really want us dead. Her sons are the most important things in her world, and she wants them all to be happy, which means married with children. She just doesn't communicate very well. It does get easier as the years go by."

Constance groaned. "Years. Lovely. It'll take years."

Judy patted Constance's back as she put water on for tea. She also had a coffee pot going on the back burner. "Do you prefer coffee or tea?"

"Tea. By far. I can't force myself to drink coffee yet."

"Does it bother you that Leonard works so late?" Judy asked.

"Not at all. I prefer to be awake later and sleep later myself, so I am happy he lives that schedule." Constance carefully used the knife Judy provided to touch up the frosting. "There. Looks good as new."

Judy nodded. "It's a beautiful cake. Mine always come out flat. That's why I asked Ma Berry to bake for us today. I do wish she hadn't insisted upon coming."

"It'll all be fine," Constance said, not sure if she was trying to convince herself or Judy.

There was a slow stream of women and children arriving after that, and Constance was pleased she'd been there first. It gave her a chance to speak with each of the ladies as they entered the house.

Last was Mrs. Berry, looking around her as if nothing was quite good enough. "You need to use more lye in your mop water, Judy. This house...well, it looks like it hasn't been mopped in weeks."

"I mopped it right after I put the children down for a nap, Ma Berry."

Constance looked around her. The house was clean. It wasn't immaculate as Mrs. Berry's was, but considering she had children underfoot at all times it looked wonderful. "I think you do a great job," Constance said.

A hush fell over the room at Constance's words, and she realized she'd spoken out of turn.

"Are you contradicting me, child?" Mrs. Berry asked.

"No, ma'am. I was simply offering a different point of view." Constance knew she was going to have a harder time with her mother-in-law because of her words, but she felt the women needed to stand up for one another.

"Don't get cheeky with me. You're the daughter, and I'm the mother. And I don't want you to forget it."

"Yes, ma'am." Constance thought she'd gotten off lightly in that exchange and vowed to try her best to do better at least for the rest of the day.

As she watched the children who came were carried upstairs for naps, while the women whose children were in school stayed downstairs and talked amongst themselves.

Soon they were all sitting around the table, and Judy had poured drinks for all of them. When she brought the cake out, it was obvious everyone was focused on the cake, worried that Ma Berry would take issue with it.

"Why is there a hole in the middle of that cake?" Mrs. Berry asked Constance, seeming annoyed.

"It's an angel food cake, which is my very favorite. I haven't made one for Leonard yet, so you'll have to tell me if it's good enough for him."

"Are you getting cheeky again?"

"Not at all. I really do want your opinion." Back east, Constance had won ribbons for her cakes at two different fairs. She'd gone against women who had been homemakers for forty years, and still her cake was the best.

Judy cut the cake into wedges and split it between the eight of them. Ma Berry received the first piece, but Judy kept serving the cake all around. Once they had their pieces, they all watched as Ma Berry took her first bite.

After a moment, Mrs. Berry nodded. "You bake a fine cake, Constance. You may serve it to Leonard."

"That's good, because I baked two and left one at home." Constance cut into her own cake, letting the flavors drift off her tongue. She'd passed her first test. Maybe Leonard didn't think she was being tested, but he was wrong. Her mother-in-law was deciding if she was good enough for her son.

Chapter Eight

After Mrs. Berry left, the other women looked at Constance. "I can't believe you got away with that," Betty said.

Constance sighed. "I didn't mean to contradict her. I just felt the need to stand up for Judy who invited us all over for tea, and whose house really isn't dirty, no matter what Mrs. Berry says."

Caroline frowned. "She hasn't asked you to call her Ma Berry yet?"

"No."

Judy sighed. "She will. And thank you for defending me, but don't feel like you need to put yourself in that situation again. I can handle her insults. I have for years."

"But she shouldn't be insulting you or anyone else. Why does she do that?"

The sisters all looked at each other. "I don't know why she does it," said Annie, one of the softer-spoken women. "She's just...well, she doesn't seem to be happy. I feel sorry for her most of the time."

"You're much kinder than I am," Constance said. "I can't stand to be treated that way, and I don't think any of you should either."

Judy patted her shoulder as she passed her to go into the kitchen and clean up their mess from tea. "I don't think you're going to be able to change her."

"But shouldn't one of us try?" Constance looked at all the other women. "Have any of you stood up to her? Am I the first?"

Betty nodded. "I love Peter too much to make him unhappy."

"I feel the same about Luke," Caroline added.

"I guess that's where I'm different from all of you. I'm not in love with Leonard...not yet anyway. I want to be, and I hope he'll love me, but I only met him a week ago. I don't want him to be unhappy, but I'm not afraid to stand up to him or his mother." Constance was afraid she was coming across as uncaring, but she wasn't sure how to get her point across if she didn't.

"I think you'll love him soon," Annie said. "You have a good heart. We can all see that. And we all appreciate you standing up for us, but I don't want you to make it worse for yourself. You never know what she'll do when she's confronted that way."

"I suppose we're going to find out whether we want to or not," Constance said. "I'll try to be kinder. I guess I need to look at her and think of her as someone who is unhappy, and try to find a way to make her happy, instead of arguing with her opinions of things."

"You get to make the choice," Betty said. "None of us are going to fault you for doing what you feel is right."

Constance sighed. "Right now, I feel it's right for me to wash the dishes."

Annie smiled. "I'll wipe them."

"I'll clear the table," Betty said.

Together the women made short work of returning the house to its clean state. When it was finished, Constance thanked Judy for the invitation. "I need to head home. I have no idea what I'm making for midnight meal tonight."

Judy gaped at Constance. "You make Leonard a meal at midnight? You're spoiling him!"

"With the way I talk to his mother, maybe that's for the best." With that, Constance headed out, untying the horse she'd ridden from the tree in the front yard. She wanted to say it was her horse, but she had a feeling Leonard would take exception to that.

All the way home, she thought about her rudeness to her mother-in-law, but she just couldn't make herself feel badly for it. The woman needed to be stood up to so she would stop treating everyone poorly. And if no one else was going to do it, she was.

*****

Constance had a beef pot pie on the table when Leonard came in from work. "Something smells good!" he called from the front door, where he hung his hat and coat.

"I hope it tastes good," Constance said, walking to the door and kissing him in greeting.

"Oh, it will," he said, grinning. "I am thrilled with your cooking. Even when you make something I'm not particularly fond of, it's still better than other women make."

"Thank you." Constance went into the kitchen and served them each a piece of the pot pie. "I'm not sure how you feel about pot pies, but I did make this one with beef."

"I appreciate that. I hope there are carrots and potatoes too. Those are my favorite pot pies."

"Yes, they're both in there."

Constance watched as he ate his first bite. When he smiled and nodded before saying, "This is delicious. You may make this every night for a month."

"Oh good. I'm glad you like it."

"I do enjoy your cooking, I just really don't enjoy chicken and dumplings very often."

"I understand," she said, though she wished things were different. "How was work today?"

"Same as usual. I did my deliveries. All went well. How was tea?"

"It was nice. Judy's house is beautiful, and my cake went over well. Your mother said it was good enough to feed you, so I can serve dessert tonight. I made two cakes."

"It must be really good if she said you could feed it to me!"

He obviously didn't understand sarcasm, but it didn't matter too terribly much. "Let me know when you're ready for some. Have you had an angel food cake?"

He shook his head. "No. I haven't."

"They're my favorite, and I've won blue ribbons for mine at fairs back east."

"Then I'm excited to try it."

"I hope you love it as much as I do."

Once he was finished eating, she cut the cake, and served them each a piece. It was her second piece of cake that day, and her mother would tell her she was going to be fat if she kept eating that way, but she didn't care. She never gained an ounce. She was more likely to be too thin.

He took three bites before pausing to take a breath. "This cake is wonderful." He finished off his piece and looked at the cake setting there on the table. "Would it be too much to ask for another piece or six?"

She laughed. "How about one? That way we'll have some tomorrow as well."

"Sounds reasonable. At the moment, I don't care about reason. I want more cake!"

Putting another piece of cake on his plate, she nodded. "I had two today, so you should get two pieces as well."

While he devoured his second piece, she cleared the table and started to work on the dishes. It seemed that all she did was clean, but she'd expected that as a wife. Her mother had taught her to be prepared for this life of hers, and she was pleased she knew how to do the important things.

"I'm going to the church for the quilting circle tomorrow afternoon," she said.

He nodded. "I thought you would. I don't know if any of my brother's wives go, but you should meet other people as well."

"I did have a lovely afternoon with all of the ladies, but it would be nice to know a few other women as well."

"And the church is the right place to meet God-fearing folks. Yes, it makes a lot of sense for you to go to the church and be part of the quilting circle."

"I'll have your afternoon meal ready before I leave and make sure your lunch pail is packed for work. Don't worry that I'll let you starve." Sometimes she thought cooking and making love were the only things he cared about where she was concerned. Those and that she was accepting of his mother, whose behavior was unacceptable by any standards.

"I would like that." He stood. "I'll wait for you in the parlor."

After finishing the dishes, Constance joined him, doing some mending while he read. He looked up from his book after a while. "Now that you know the sisters-in-law, do you miss your family less?"

She gaped at him. The man was completely clueless about a woman's emotions. What was wrong with him? "No, I don't miss them less. If anything, I miss them more. Spending time with everyone today made me think about how different it would have been with my family."

"Just keep getting to know everyone, and soon you won't think of your family at all." With that, he went back to reading the paper, while Constance quietly seethed beside him.

*****

Constance felt a little shy as she arrived at the church the following day. The only woman she knew in town was the pastor's wife, and she didn't see Mrs. Abrams when she looked around the room. None of her sisters-in-law were there either.

There was an empty seat beside a woman who looked as if she was in her last month before her baby was born. Constance took the seat, hoping no one would ask her to move. She felt out of place in a way she never had before.

The pregnant woman smiled at her. "You're new here. I saw you sitting with Leonard Berry at church on Sunday. I'm Abigail by the way."

"I'm Leonard's wife, Constance Berry. It's nice to meet you."

"I won't be able to come to these much longer, so I'm enjoying the quilting circle while I can."

Constance smiled. "When are you due?"

"Three more weeks, though the midwife keeps telling me the first babe is usually slow to come."

"A first baby is so exciting. Do you want a boy or girl?"

"Oh, I'd like a girl for me, so I could teach her all about being a lady, but for my husband, I want a boy. He needs help around the farm." Abigail shrugged. "I guess that means I'd be happy with either a boy or girl."

"I guess it does. Well, I think it's wonderful. Do you have everything ready?"

"I hope so. My mother is coming from Rhode Island after the baby is born. She's so excited to be a grandmother. I just wish she'd be closer so she could really know him or her."

"How long have you been away from your family?" Constance asked, thinking what it would be like to be pregnant and not have her mother around. She didn't like the idea one whit.

"Bob and I got married eighteen months ago, and I moved out here to be with him after that. He'd always loved the idea of having a farm, and I went along with it. Now I want my mother."

"I know I would feel the same way if I were you."

"Bob wanted to be here for the free land, and I couldn't argue with the price. So here we are. I'm just thankful there's a train coming through here so my mother can visit easily. As long as she doesn't mind spending a week on a train of course."

Constance covered the other woman's hand with hers. "If you need help between now and your mother's arrival, you just let me know. I'm happy to fix meals or help around your home. I have plenty of time. My husband works at night."

"I may have to take you up on that. Bob doesn't think I should need help, but the babe is getting so big it's hard to do anything. I know if

I was a good wife, I'd just be able to push through it all and do what needs to be done, but it's so hard for me."

"I will be there anytime you need me. I would love to help you."

"Then I will not be afraid to ask if I really need it."

Mrs. Abrams hurried in then, taking the only empty seat in the circle. "Let's start with a prayer, and then I'll introduce our new member."

After the prayer, she nodded to Constance. "Constance Berry recently came here from Massachusetts to marry Leonard Berry. She'll be joining our sewing circle, and she is of course, now part of the huge Berry clan that seems to be taking over our part of South Dakota."

Everyone laughed, and Constance smiled. "Thanks for the introduction, Mrs. Abrams."

They went in a circle and each woman gave her name and told one thing about herself. Most said things related to their husbands. "I'm a farmer's wife," or "I'm Doc Braddock's wife."

When it came time for Constance to say something, she mentioned Leonard and told how she'd come to town as a mail-order bride. Many of the women seemed intrigued at the idea.

"I'll be asking you more about that later," Abigail said.

"I'm happy to answer any questions."

After that, they mostly talked to their neighbors. "Are you happy here?" Abigail asked.

"I'm afraid to answer that prematurely," Constance said. "Leonard is a good man, and I think I will be happy, but I don't know just yet."

"I hope you love it here. I still don't know how I feel about South Dakota. I miss my home and family so much." Abigail's hand went to her burgeoning belly. "Especially now."

"We'll have to decide and let each other know the answer."

After the quilting circle, Constance went to the butcher to pick up meat for the next couple of nights. She'd decided on a beef stew for that night, knowing it would please Leonard to have beef again. It was a good thing he made good money, because his love for beef wasn't as economical as she would have chosen to eat.

When she got home, she started the laundry. She knew it would be better to do during the day, but these were her hours to work, and she was going to take care of her wash.

By the time Leonard was home from work, the stew was ready, and she was very tired. Her mother had always handled the wash, and she'd helped. It had never been her chore before, and she realized that day how hard it really was. Washing, then rinsing, and then hanging everything on the line had her exhausted before she'd even started to cook their midnight meal.

Leonard came home to the smell of beef stew, and he let his nose carry him to the kitchen. "That smells absolutely delicious. I don't know how you manage to make something good every single night."

She smiled, going to the table with their bowls of stew. "I probably won't be up terribly late tonight. I did the laundry today, and I've never done wash by myself before."

"Are your arms sore?" he asked. He knew his mother had always had sore arms after doing the wash.

"Yes, they are. I'll be all right though. As long as I can go to bed early."

"Then that's exactly what you should do."

Chapter Nine

As the next few weeks went by, Constance was more and more attached to Leonard, but she kept a part of herself distant as well. He had such strange ideas about her adopting his family as her own that she wasn't sure if they could be completely compatible...but whether they were or not, she knew she was in love with him.

A note was delivered to their door shortly after they woke up on a Thursday and when Constance read it, she couldn't help but smile. "My friend, Abigail, had her baby. The midwife wants her to rest as much as possible for a few days, so I'm going to go over and help her with her cleaning and cooking. I'll take care of my chores here first, but I'll spend a lot of time helping them."

Leonard frowned. "It's good to help a neighbor, but I like knowing my wife is here waiting for me."

"I promised I would help if she needed me. You don't want me to break my promise, do you?"

He shook his head. "No, but next time you should check with me before you promise something like that."

Constance bit her tongue, which had become a common practice in the time she'd been in South Dakota. She simply gathered the things she would need to help, and prepared to go.

Leonard sighed. "You really don't think you need my permission, do you?"

"To help a neighbor and do my duty as a Christian? Not at all. You may be my head, but God is yours, and I follow him first."

He frowned at her. "You really shouldn't speak to me that way."

Constance raised on tiptoes to kiss his cheek. "I'm taking the buggy out to their place. I'll be home in time to make our midnight meal." She walked out the front door then, carrying the things she'd need.

Leonard stared at the door for a moment before following his wife. "I'll hitch up the buggy for you."

She smiled at him. "Thank you." She thought he may be coming around to her way of thinking when he followed, but there was no way to be certain. The man confused her regularly.

As she drove to the farm Abigail shared with her husband, she thought hard about her marriage and whether it was the right thing for her. She didn't believe in divorce, but even though she loved the man, he didn't seem to take her thoughts and feelings into account. He still didn't think she should miss her family, which she felt was utter nonsense.

By the time she arrived at Abigail's, Constance thought maybe she'd figured things out. She needed to have a long talk with Leonard and tell him exactly how she felt about his dismissing her thoughts and feelings. If he did it again, perhaps it would be time for her to buy a train ticket back to Beckham. It would bring shame on her family if she couldn't make her marriage work, but there was no reason for her to be miserable for the rest of her life with a man who didn't even try to understand her.

She knocked on the door of Abigail's farm, thankful her friend had given her explicit instructions on how to get there. Abigail called, "Come in!"

Constance walked inside and found her friend looking as if she hadn't slept in a week in her rocking chair with the baby. "Boy or girl?" she asked, looking down at the sleeping child.

"Girl. We named her Charlotte."

"What a beautiful name for a beautiful child." Constance looked around her. "When did you last eat?" There was a great deal of cleaning to be done, but it was more important for her friend to eat than be in a clean environment.

"Last night?" Abigail looked confused.

"I'll make a meal first then. Has your husband eaten?"

"Mark? No, I don't think he has..."

"Then I'll fix a meal and go outside to call him to see if he's hungry as well." Constance looked at how frail Abigail seemed. She was worried about her. "After you've eaten, perhaps you should sleep for a while. I can bring you the baby if she cries. I'll take care of everything else."

"Thank you."

Constance hurriedly made a simple meal for her friend and her husband, calling Mark to come in and eat when she was finished. "Aren't you going to eat with us?" Abigail asked.

"No, I'm not. I'm going to keep cleaning. I had my meal with Leonard before I left town."

She had no qualms about changing the sheets on the bed and getting it made up properly for her friend's much needed nap. Once that was finished, she walked into the main room of their small cabin and saw that Abigail was finished eating and nursing the baby. There was a small wooden cradle in one corner of the room, and Constance took the baby and placed her in it while Abigail went to sleep.

As soon as everyone was quiet, Constance rushed around the room, picking up things that had lain where they'd fallen for who knew how long. Abigail obviously hadn't had the strength to do more than she had.

She wished there was time to get baking, cooking, cleaning, and laundry done before she left, but she knew that a quick clean and food was what was needed most.

Constance made a stew that could be reheated for their noon meal the next day, and even for breakfast if they needed to. She went out and collected eggs from the chickens, and milked the cow. Mark was off in the fields making sure his crops didn't die, so he hadn't seen to either of those things as he should have. She guessed it was normally Abigail's job, so he hadn't thought to do it. The man looked almost as tired as his wife.

By the time Mark came in for the evening, there were two loaves of fresh bread, a pot of stew, and fresh milk. She'd even made a cake for their dessert that evening. "I think you're going to have to wake Abigail if you want to eat with her."

He nodded, going into the bedroom, which was really a small area of the house with a sheet that pulled closed.

Looking around her, Constance mapped out the following day and the chores that would need to be done. Another meal, mopping, and laundry. She thought laundry may just be the most important thing she could do for them. She wasn't sure how old little Charlotte was, but there was an impressive amount of dirty diapers.

When Mark and Abigail came out, Abigail smiled at her friend. "You have done so much! Thank you."

"Is there anything else I can do before I head home? I plan to mop, do laundry, and cook more tomorrow."

"That's perfect," Abigail said. "We appreciate your help so much."

On her way, Constance rehearsed the conversation she wanted to have with her husband that night. She wanted to make him understand that she couldn't just forget about her family and move on as if his family were hers. She needed him to know that she missed her mother a great deal, and his could never take her place.

She did her chores that night mindlessly, thinking only about trying to talk to Leonard. He'd made things difficult so far, and though she understood he didn't know better, she needed him to learn to treat her better than he had so far. She wasn't going to be able to stay married to a man who didn't at least try to understand her feelings.

She made roast beef and mashed potatoes, which she knew was Leonard's favorite meal, and a loaf of yesterday's bread.

When Leonard came in that evening, she could immediately tell it wasn't the night for their conversation. He'd obviously had a hard day at work. "What happened?" she asked.

He groaned. "What didn't happen? I broke a wheel and had to change it in the dark, which is never particularly easy, and one of the horses was feeling cantankerous. It was a hard night all together."

"I'm sorry. Does it help that I made your favorite meal?"

"That always helps." He wrapped his arms around her and held her close for a moment. "You are the brightest spot in my day."

She rested her head on his shoulder, feeling a little better with his words. "I'm glad."

"How are your friend and the baby?" he asked.

"She's exhausted. I'm a little worried about her. The baby seems to be doing fine. It's a little girl they named Charlotte."

"I like that name!"

"I do too." She walked into the kitchen, well aware that Leonard was following her. "I did a quick clean, but there needs to be more. I don't think she was able to do her spring cleaning this year. I'll catch up her normal cleaning and laundry tomorrow, but I think I'm going to have to do her spring cleaning as well. I'll be going out on Saturday and Sunday so I can make sure they eat. Abigail couldn't remember for sure the last time she'd eaten."

He frowned. "It sounds like they need a lot of help. Do you think Mark would like my company in the fields? The first few years out here are so hard, I'd like to be able to do what I can to help."

"I think they would appreciate that a great deal. I know farming isn't your favorite thing, but it's worth it to help a neighbor."

He nodded. "It is. I always feel so good after helping someone that way. I know I'll be happy once I've done it."

"Good. I'll let them know you're planning to help."

He sat at the table and gratefully accepted the food she served. "Thank you. Maybe this will help my mood a little. It really was a hard day."

"I hope it does. I mixed a little bit of honey into the butter today. It'll help make the day-old bread taste perfect."

"I appreciate how you always think about me and try to put me first. I know it's not always easy with other people needing you as well."

"You're my husband," she said simply, thinking that explained everything. A good wife always saw to her husband's needs before doing anything else.

"I thank God for that fact every day."

Constance smiled at that. "We're going to be able to have a wonderful marriage if we work on it together."

"Work? Our marriage is perfect just the way it is."

Constance didn't respond to that, because she didn't know what to say. They did need to work on their marriage. Of course they did. She needed to know that he was thinking of her and her feelings. He needed to know she would never be able to accept another family to take the place of her own. But now wasn't the time for that discussion. It would wait until tomorrow.

Chapter Ten

It was late morning on Saturday when Leonard and Constance drove out to Mark and Abigail's farm. While they drove, they talked about ways they could help the other couple. "I'm going to make enough food for today and tomorrow, so we don't have to come back until Monday."

"That's a good idea. I don't know what kind of help Mark needs, but there are always several men needed on a homestead, and I know they have no hired hands. I'll do whatever is necessary to help out." He sighed. "I hate farming."

"It's a good thing you don't do it then, isn't it?"

When they got to the farm, she headed into the house, and Leonard went in search of Mark. She was surprised to see Abigail sitting at the table, looking a great deal better than she had. "You look good today!" Constance said.

"I must have looked awful before then." Abigail shook her head.

"You looked tired. Now, tell me what I can fix for you and Mark to eat today and tomorrow."

"I sent Mark into town to get a few things, so it'll be much easier. We love what you've come up with, so just look through the food we have, and make a decision." Abigail hid a yawn behind her hand.

"Do you need a nap?" Constance asked. "My ma always says to sleep when the baby is sleeping."

"I feel like I've done nothing but sleep for days. I need to do something."

"You can keep me company while I cook and clean. It's the perfect answer. I want to do as much of your spring cleaning as I can today, so you won't have to worry about that as you feel better."

Abigail's eyes widened. "I couldn't ask you to do that!"

"You don't have to ask. I'm offering. I always helped my ma with it, and someone did it before I arrived, so I feel like it's not really spring. Help me to know it's the right season!"

Abigail laughed at her friend. "You talked me into it."

Constance started by taking down the sheet that hung between the bedroom and the rest of the house, taking it outside to brush and hang, getting the cleansing power of the sun. Then she dragged out the mattress and the bed itself, scrubbing them down, using a feather in each small hole in the bedstead.

Once that was finished, she scrubbed the walls and floor in the bedroom. "Is it all right if I don't whitewash the ceiling?" she asked Abigail. "I fear that would leave your home upended, and I don't plan to return until Monday."

"Please skip the whitewashing. I can do that as part of my fall cleaning this year."

"Then your bedroom is done other than the windows, which I'll do all at once, and the bed being brought back inside. I think I got every bit of dust out of it."

Abigail smiled. "I appreciate all you're doing, but you really don't have to."

"Of course, I don't. I do it with love for my friend." And she started on the floor in the main room. The house was tiny, so it was no real inconvenience to do the spring cleaning for her.

By the end of the day, the windows were washed, all the floors and walls scrubbed, and the stove blackened. There was nothing that didn't look shiny and new but the ceiling, and that could easily be taken care of with the fall cleaning.

When it was suppertime, the two men came into the house, and Constance scolded them both to remove their boots before stepping indoors. "I put too much time into scrubbing these floors to have the two of you spread dirt everywhere before the sun even sets."

Both men took their boots off and left them on the front stoop, before walking in to wash their hands with the water pump. They sat down, and Mark said their prayer, thanking God for sending such wonderful friends to them.

Abigail seemed awfully tired after sitting in her chair awake all day, but she still seemed better than she had the previous two days. "I don't think you'll need to come back on Monday," Abigail said to Constance. "You've done so much, and I'm getting my strength back."

"All right, but if you change your mind, have Mark bring me a note, and I'll be here as fast as I can."

Before they left, Leonard looked at Mark. "We're going to go choose one."

Mark nodded. "We certainly don't need them all."

"Choose what?" Constance asked.

Leonard just smiled, taking her hand and pulling her out the door and toward the barn. Once inside, he led her to an empty stall, and there she saw what he meant. Four small kittens. "Mark says they're all weaned, and we just need to choose which we want."

Constance clapped her hands together, excited that he'd remembered her request from her first week in Sioux Falls. "They're adorable!"

"Well, pick one! I want to get home before midnight!"

"Why?" she asked, cheekily. "You are never home before midnight!"

He chuckled. "Just pick a kitten."

"How old are they?" she asked, sinking down on the straw and looking at the fluffy little creatures.

"Mark said eight weeks. So they're ready for new homes now."

"Oh, I want them all!" Reaching out, she picked a little calico kitten up and tucked it under her chin. When the kitten purred she smiled. "I want this one."

Leonard took the kitten from her, turning it over onto its back. "It's a female."

"All right." Constance looked at him. "Is this one the one you want?"

He shrugged. "I don't care one way or the other."

"Then I'm taking this one. Thank you for arranging this for me!"

"I thought it might make you a little less lonely for your family."

Her breath caught as she stared at him. "You understand I'm lonely for my family now?"

He nodded. "I can't expect you to forget where you came from just because you're here with me now. I'm sorry if I made you feel like you weren't allowed to miss them."

Tears sprang to her eyes. He finally seemed to understand. Finally. He may never understand about his mother, but that was all right. She could deal with a persnickety mother-in-law, as long as she had a happy marriage otherwise. "Thank you."

Taking the kitten back from him, she cradled it close to her, keeping her eyes averted. She didn't want him to know she was crying. It would be hard to explain.

Cuddling the kitten the entire way home, she thought about what to name the beautiful little kitten. Finally, she came up with a name that seemed to fit the sweet creature. "I'm going to call her Felicity. Because she makes me happy."

"That's a perfect name for her." Leonard truly didn't care about the kitten's name, and he was still unsure about having her in the house, but she made Constance so happy, and that was important to him.

Once they were in the house, she set a shallow crate out for the kitten to do her business in, and pulled in some dirt from the backyard, until they could find some sand. Then she found two small bowls in the kitchen, filling one with water, and the other with meat.

The kitten had no trouble knowing what to do with those things, and she hurried to the water bowl, slurping at the liquid, and falling face first into the water, which made Constance giggle.

"I'll have to make her a pillow to use for a bed."

Leonard shook his head. "They just use straw in a barn."

"But she's not a barn cat. She's a little princess."

He chuckled. "I'm glad you're happy with your gift."

"I am, but not just because of the kitten." She walked into the parlor and sat on the sofa, waiting for him to join her. "The kitten is symbolic."

"How is a kitten symbolic?" he asked, his brows drawn together.

"You've told me over and over that I should forget about my family because I have yours here. When you gave me the kitten, you said that it was to help me with my loneliness for my family. I was starting to feel as if you didn't care about my feelings at all."

Leonard frowned. "I do care about your feelings."

"I know that now. I was thinking about buying a train ticket back to my family, because I wasn't sure I could live with a man who discounted my feelings so quickly, even though I love him."

"Wait...You love me?" Leonard asked, a smile spreading slowly across his face.

"Of course I love you! Do you think I'd have put up with you for this long if I didn't?"

He chuckled. "I guess I'm not perfect..."

"No one is." She sighed. "I can easily deal with how your mother treats me, as long as I know I have your love!"

"I've seen Ma with you. She treats you just like she does her other daughters-in-law. She loves you!"

Constance shrugged, not willing to argue about it when she felt like she'd just won a huge victory. "If you say so."

"I love you, Constance," Leonard said softly. "I know you think my brothers' have more romantic stories about how they got together with their wives than we do, but I think ours is special. You are the woman I imagined when I wrote that letter asking for a bride, and I've been happy with you since the moment you arrived."

She frowned at him. "But you didn't *choose* me."

"Perhaps not, but I choose to keep you and to love you. You are the woman I want beside me every day of my life."

She wrapped her arms around him and pulled him down for a kiss. "And I choose to love you every day."

He sighed happily.

Epilogue

Constance struggled into a sitting position on her bed, Abigail and Caroline at her side. "He's beautiful," Abigail whispered.

Constance looked down at the baby in her arms, trying to fathom how this little miracle of life could possibly be hers. "The most beautiful baby in the world," she said softly.

Caroline smiled. "I agree. But in a month, I get to have the most beautiful baby in the world."

"I suppose I could agree with that." Constance reached out and squeezed Caroline's hand, not able to quite reach Abigail. "Thank you for being here for the birth."

"I owe you so much," Abigail said. "I never would have made it through after the baby was born without you."

Felicity peeked her head up over the bottom of the bed, staring at Constance. She'd obviously been frightened by the screams she heard. "I'm okay Felicity. I promise."

With the reassurance the cat ran off to the other room. "We need to go get Leonard and Ma Berry," Caroline said. "They're going to want to see the baby...and know its gender."

"Yes, they will. Thank you for coming when the midwife couldn't. I panicked a great deal in those first minutes." Constance shook her head. "How dare someone else go into labor right before me?"

Abigail laughed softly. "It worked out. We were here for you."

Abigail and Caroline left the room to fetch Leonard and Ma Berry. When Leonard came in, she could see the worry on his face. "I'm fine. And the baby—your son—is perfect. He has ten fingers and ten toes and a set of lungs that will keep us up far too many nights."

Leonard sat beside her on the bed, gazing at their son, while Ma Berry stood over them. "I'll be seeing to your meals for three days. It takes that long to recover from giving birth. After that, you'll see to your own family."

"Thank you," Constance said. She had been warned by the other sisters that this would be her only gift upon the birth of her child from Ma Berry. "I really appreciate it."

"I'll stay in one of the upstairs rooms until you are capable of caring for Leonard and the boy on your own." With that, Ma Berry left the room.

Leonard shook his head. "She didn't even ask what we're going to name him."

"I know she didn't. That's all right. What shall we name him?" Constance asked. She'd finally gotten used to his mother, and she could tolerate her ways.

"I'd like to name him either Michael after my father, or David, after your father."

Constance smiled. "I like both names. Let's name this one Michael, and the next boy will be David."

"You're willing to have another baby?" he asked. "I'm not sure I'm ready for that. You were in such pain! I could hear your screams from outside."

"Of course, I'll have another. I barely remember the pain. The baby made the whole world melt away as soon as I held him. Michael. Michael Leonard Berry."

"Thank you for my son!"

"I hope we can have many more."

Don't miss out!

Visit the website below and you can sign up to receive emails whenever Kirsten Osbourne publishes a new book. There's no charge and no obligation.

https://books2read.com/r/B-A-VSFD-CZRXB

BOOKS 2 READ

Connecting independent readers to independent writers.